BETWEEN MEMORY AND OBLIVION

BETWEEN MEMORY AND OBLIVION

A NOVEL

PETER BRISCOE

PALO VERDE PRESS

Published by Palo Verde Press

18608 Oak Park Drive

Riverside, California 92504

Cover designed by Aleksndar Milosavljevic Alek of 99designs

ISBN 978-0-9634898-6-9

eISBN 978-0-9634898-3-8

For Lori

His purpose was to strip Venice of what remained and to reduce the people and all those who read to ABCs and prayer books. Nothing displeased him. All, he found good, especially books written by unknown authors.

—Ismaël Boulliau to Jacques and Pierre Dupuy,
December 15, 1645

1

Michael Ashe knew his way around the library. He considered it his second office. After returning from his most recent book buying trip, he was spending a week there looking up details about the titles he had purchased. He was working in the Main Reference Room, which was grand. A cathedral of knowledge. Although its collection had been steadily shrinking to make space for more computer terminals, it still contained the mother lode of bibliographic reference sources. Those he had pulled from the shelves to consult were strewn across a large table, where he sat by himself, hunched over, annotating a stack of index cards. The card in his hand read:

Palacios, Enrique Juan

En los confines de la selva lacandona: exploraciones en el estado de Chiapas, mayo-agosto, 1926. México, D. F.: Secretaría de Educación Pública, 1928.

215 p., maps, color plates, photos, tall 4to, in wraps (backstrip torn). Condition otherwise excellent.

The report of an important archaeological expedition into the rain forest of Chiapas.

HE PAUSED FOR A MOMENT. What no one else seemed to know was that the expedition's photographer was the mysterious figure B. Traven, a German anarchist, fugitive, and author of several terrific novels about Mexico, including *The Treasure of the Sierra Madre.* As usual, Traven was working under a pseudonym. This fact, uncovered by the East German scholar Rolf Recknagel —Michael glanced at his notes, *B. Traven: Beiträge zur Biographie,* 1966, pp. 204-207—doubled the value of the book. He added this information to the card as well as the price, now $500. He smiled. George was going to love this one.

Maybe it was time to go see George, to whet his appetite, and set up a future appointment. George Rosen was a senior librarian in the Collection Development Department, a history and foreign languages bibliographer who covered a dazzling array of subjects.

He had a generous book budget, reflecting the status of the university as a flagship of the state's higher education system. He had studied European History, earning a Ph.D. and later a library degree. His graduate work emphasized the discovery and colonization of the New World. He spoke fluent Spanish and read in several others. When younger he had bummed around Latin America and Europe. Now in his late fifties, he was physically a big man, energetic but a little clumsy. He wore glasses and had a beard. Known as a fine raconteur, his stories were hilarious. Booming laughter usually announced that he was in the vicinity.

Even though the library had a collection of several million volumes, there was still much of value that it lacked. George worked with a number of antiquarian booksellers like Michael to bring in choice titles and special collections. These booksellers were experts in the bibliography of their subjects. Once they knew the collecting interests of a library, they would search for and channel uncommon titles to it. George peppered them with lists of desiderata, and he was such a regular, reliable, and knowledgeable buyer that he was always given the right of first refusal and a discount.

Michael slipped a rubber band around his stack of index cards, pushed back from the table, and threaded his way across the Reference Room, nodding to the young librarian on duty at the desk. The offices of the bibliographers were not far away. George's door was closed, so he knocked. A moment later a woman opened the door. She was about thirty, nice looking, and well dressed.

"May I help you?"

"Pardon me, but I was looking for George Rosen. Has he changed offices?"

She stared at him, then said, "George retired."

"What? That really surprises me. He didn't say a thing the last time I saw him. This is awful news."

"Yes, it happened quickly."

"May I ask why? And I should probably introduce myself. My name is Michael Ashe. I'm a bookseller, and I've known George for many years. Where is he now?"

"I'm not certain, but I believe he returned to the East Coast. Boston, I think. I was appointed to replace him, but he left before I came. The Personnel Office can probably give you his forwarding address."

"Well, I'm stunned. George was a wonderful librarian. I worked with him for years, and sold him hundreds of books, even whole collections. In fact, I came by today to make an appointment to show him my latest finds, including some books he had been seeking for a long time. They are perfect for this library. Are you the one I should show them to now?"

"I suppose so, but I can't promise anything."

She looked at him for a moment, then added: "I have assumed George's responsibilities, but there is much more to my job than that. I am also the Digital Resources Librarian. My appointment was pending when George decided to leave, so they asked me to do his job too, at least for the time being. I'm sorry to say this, but I'm not ready to see the books you're offering. Not until I understand the budget better, and not until we rethink the collection development policy. The Director would like that to be my first priority."

"I see, now is not a good time. There's something else which I hesitate to mention, having just met you, but it may be a while before I see you again. For the last few years I've been putting together an unusual collection—a special collection—intended for this library. It's about French scientists and savants in Latin America. George encouraged me after he saw the beginnings of it in my place of business. I've been keeping my eyes open and adding to it and recently had the luck to acquire a cache of very early and rare titles from the wife of a deceased professor. With this, the collection has achieved a critical mass. I was going to offer it to George."

"Oh, Mr. Ashe, I'm sure that kind of acquisition

would be out of the question. Not with our budget problems. And it's not where the library is going."

He glanced down. "Okay, I guess that's it. Good luck on your new job."

Feeling almost ill, Michael hurried down the hall to a stairwell that led to the Acquisitions Department in the basement—a large, brightly lit room with desks and worktables in the center and small offices around the perimeter. About ten clerks, working at computer terminals, were ordering or receiving new acquisitions, pulling them off book carts parked beside their desks. He spotted Walt Fisher standing in the middle of the room talking to a coworker, caught his attention, and pointed to his office. Walt, dressed in jeans, was a senior library assistant, known for his competence and wit, who often took coffee with George.

They shook hands. "Michael, good to see you. It's been quite a while."

"Yeah, I've been traveling a lot, and I'm again between trips. Just back from Mexico, and about to go to Paris."

"Oh, such a rough life! Need an assistant?"

"Sorry, business just took a dive. That's why I came to see you. Where's George? There's this young blonde in his office."

"Elizabeth Wyatt. Yes, she's quite a looker—but all

business. To answer your question, there's been a regime change. New director, who intends to greatly speed up the shift to electronics. George protested, said a lot more than he ought to have, and quit. Elizabeth, his replacement, sees things a different way. Almost opposite."

"I'm screwed."

AN HOUR later Michael opened the door of his condominium, which was located in the quiet foothill town of Sierra Madre, just east of Pasadena. After months of house hunting he had lucked out in finding this place: a two-bedroom, Spanish Revival apartment, circa 1925, part of a small complex that had been refurbished then sold as condominiums. He shared its lush, shady courtyard and trickling Moorish fountain with his neighbors.

The interior was equally agreeable. White plaster walls, dark wooden beams, arched doorways, and wrought iron hardware. He had furnished the front room with pieces from New Mexico, accented by a luminous R. C. Gorman lithograph of a Navajo woman grinding corn. Strangely, the apartment contained few books. In the kitchen there was a shelf of culinary classics and in his bedroom, a shelf of dictionaries and grammars in English, French, and Spanish, as well as a half dozen books he was currently reading, which were stacked on the floor beside the bed.

Unlike many of his confrères, Michael was an avid reader. But after a few years of being a bookseller he understood that he also needed relief from his business: from scanning thousands of offers in booksellers' catalogs, from opening box after box of dusty books in hot garages, and especially from being surrounded by his own extensive stock. Stock is an ambivalent factor in a bookseller's life. At times it comforts him and is a source of pride and wealth; at other times it's terribly depressing, a burden, a crushing, disorganized mass. Michael called these feelings "book overload," and knew it to be an occupational disease. Many dealers coped by simply not reading anymore, at least for personal benefit, often preferring to drink instead. Michael coped by going home and narrowing his gaze to a single book that he could lose himself in.

After drinking a glass of water, he went straight to the bedroom. He pulled a suitcase and a carry-on bag out of the closet, spread them open on the bed, and began to pack. About an hour later, and almost finished, he paused to phone his assistant at the office.

"Hi, María, it's me. I'm at home packing. Any phone calls?"

"No one. *Como una iglesia.* When do you leave?"

"This afternoon at 6:20. Air France. You know where I'll be staying. You've got the phone number, but if something comes up, just e-mail me. It's cheaper. I may stay longer than expected, so you will have to hold down the fort."

"Oh my. Solitude. At least you have a lot of books here for me to read."

"Well, I do have something to keep you busy. When the shipment from Mexico arrives, with the books I intended to sell to George, list them on the Internet."

"My God, what happened?"

"He's gone."

2

Michael had never been able to sleep on a plane. If he dozed for a half hour during the flight he would be lucky. He liked Air France because they always had a fresh supply of French newspapers and magazines on board as a courtesy to passengers, items hard to come by in the United States. He picked out an issue each of *Le Monde, Figaro, Nouvel Observateur,* and *L'Express*. He would read these for the next eleven hours, beginning his practice of trying to think, read, and speak exclusively in French while in France. When he first started visiting the country as a college student fifteen years before, and his French was not so good, he easily became flustered. But now, at age 35, he would calmly repeat himself if not understood. He noticed that the French had become a little more tolerant of a foreigner's mistakes after they began their own struggle to learn English.

After arriving at Charles de Gaulle Airport, he claimed his luggage, passed through customs, and headed for the RER station. This train ride to the center of Paris ran through a series of rough-looking industrial suburbs. The sky was gray and people waiting on the platforms wore their jackets zipped. He felt jet-lagged and out of sorts. At Aulnay a group of *lycéens* boarded the car, and a girl in boots and a canvas coat plunked down beside him, continuing to talk on a cell phone to a friend. Her leg pressed against his from hip to ankle. It startled him, because seating wasn't that tight. The warmth of her body flooded him. He thought he should move over, but didn't, until the absurdity of never again seeing this fifteen-year-old girl hit him. Then he scooted over, and she gave him a pitiful look. The incident was nothing, but he thought about it off and on for several days.

He got off at the Luxembourg station, and emerged into the fresh cool air of a beautiful part of Paris on the Boulevard Saint-Michel, right across from the garden. He crossed over, and rolled his suitcase along the sidewalk bordering the garden until he passed the Palais du Luxembourg. Then he cut north one street to the tranquil Place Saint-Sulpice, where his favorite hotel was located. Over the years, Michael had stayed in hotels all over the city, deliberately favoring a different *arrondissement* each trip, in order to explore. This had been a good project, but he had finally settled on the Hôtel Récamier, a charming two star in the Sixth, the district where publishers and booksellers were concentrated. It was convenient for business, but he simply liked the hotel. It was a narrow building squeezed into one corner of the Place. In the tiny lobby, there was a reproduction of David's famous portrait of Madame Récamier reclining on a chaise longue. Her spirit permeated the rooms too. His had light blue wallpaper with small pink flowers illuminated by a large, double window opening onto the Place. Definitely a room a woman would like upon entering, a good place to bring a girlfriend or wife. But he liked it too. Its airy brightness was an antidote to Parisian weather.

He unpacked, took a shower, and at dusk left the hotel to find a café nearby where he ordered *steak-frites* and a half-bottle of wine. He was numb, having been up for thirty hours. At last he could sleep.

The next morning he walked down to the Seine. He leaned over the parapet watching the green-brown current, a breeze blowing through his hair. A barge passed under the Pont des Arts as pedestrians crossed over on the way to the Louvre. He turned around and headed back along the Rue Bonaparte. On this street, in proximity to the École des Beaux Arts, were a couple of dealers who specialized in out-of-print art books. The first shop he entered was unusually elegant, made more so by a beautiful young woman seated at the reception desk. This was always the case. He couldn't help thinking that, whatever her competence, she was displayed as a work of art herself, preliminary to a wide inventory of books on the subject.

"*Bonjour*, Mademoiselle."

"*Bonjour*, Monsieur. How may I help you?"

"Today, I'm looking for two Delvaux, the painter Paul and the journalist Alfred. Not related, of course, and the surnames, not even spelled the same."

"You are teasing, Monsieur. You give me a riddle. I'm sure we have much on the former and nothing on the latter. Which titles?"

He pulled out a list.

An hour later he emerged from the shop with one book, although he had arranged to have three others shipped to his office in California. The book he carried was to replace a copy stolen from a college library. It was a superb book, not really rare but becoming harder to find, and he wanted to look at it again—Michel Butor's *Delvaux: catalogue de l'œuvre peint* (1975). Some undergraduate had found these voluptuous nudes, who seem to be sleepwalking in dreamscapes, irresistible. This was a book destined to be stolen every time it was replaced. He felt he had better take another look at it while he could.

He walked on, but had no luck at the next store, so he cut over to the Rue Mazarine to a small shop specializing in theatre, spectacles, and the circus. Its proprietor, a dignified, older woman, said she did have one or two works by Alfred Delvau. Delvau lived in the mid-nineteenth century and worked as a reporter for *Figaro*. His job dovetailed perfectly with his pastime, which was roaming the city to observe its "little history," the social life of common Parisians. He wrote at least thirty books, including a dictionary of slang, a history of cafés and cabarets, an account of the 1848 Revolution (which he witnessed), and a guidebook called *Les Plaisirs de Paris*. Although research libraries in the United States generally had strong collections in French history, Michael found their holdings of Delvau to be spotty. His work was therefore easy to sell. That day Michael procured two unusual titles that would fetch a good price: *Les Dessous de Paris* (1862), which could be translated as "The Underside of Paris," and *Les Cythères parisiennes: histoire anecdotique des bals de Paris* (1864), about dance halls, illustrated with etchings by Félicien Rops.

Buying books in France for resale was tricky. The
question was: Who in the U.S. would want them?
Michael always tried to have a potential buyer in mind.
He didn't buy to keep as stock. Stock mainly consisted
of books that hadn't sold, where he had failed to judge
the market. In his hotel room at night, using a laptop,
he would check the online catalogs of libraries to see if
they already held titles he was considering. He encouraged librarians to give him lists of desiderata and lost
books, and was able to find a certain percentage. But
this was dog work, time consuming and not too prof-
itable. The most promising area was special collections,
where a library had great strength and interest. He
knew, for example, that UC Davis would never turn
down a book it didn't have on viticulture or wine
making, and that Cornell would never refuse one on
witchcraft provided the price was fair. Even so, unso-
licited offers usually had no effect. Not until he knew
someone in the library, a key bibliographer or special
collections librarian, someone who trusted his judg-
ment, was he able to sell in any consistent manner.

For the rest of the week, he continued to hunt for
books. He visited the Librairie Gaspa on the Rue de
Vaugirard for bibliography and the history of the book;
the Librairie Thomas Scheler on the Rue de Tournon
for voyage literature and early science; Fabrice Bayarré

almost next door for Latin American explorations; the Librairie Historique Jean Clavreuil on the Rue St-André-des-Arts for French history and colonial adventures; Elliot Klein just down the street for ethnology, archaeology, and linguistics, and so forth. Since the Middle Ages, Paris has been called the City of Books. At last count there were 250 shops which sold old books, and even more which sold new books. He could easily spend months there.

But results were hit and miss—actually, more miss. Typically, French antiquarian booksellers display only a tiny fraction of their stock, mostly uninteresting tomes. The customer must know what he wants, and ask for it. The dealer will be sizing him up. After he forms an opinion of the buyer's worthiness, he may or may not reveal whether he has the book. Caprice, impatience, disdain—all may influence the transaction. There will be no browsing, no serendipitous discoveries, and no jackpots until the day when—*quel mystère*—the dealer embraces the bewildered customer as a long lost comrade, asking why it has been so long since his last visit—a day which, for most, never comes. Then he becomes a friend for life, willing to show his empire.

At the end of the week, Michael took a break. There was an exposition of *Les Femmes impressionnistes: Mary Cassatt, Eva Gonzalès, Berthe Morisot* at the Musée

Marmottan that he wanted to see. This lovely museum in the Sixteenth *arrondissement*, occupying the mansion of the original collector, was undoubtedly his favorite. It never seemed to be too crowded despite being full of masterpieces. He had long admired Cassatt and Morisot, but was ignorant of Eva Gonzalès's work. She turned out to be a revelation. He decided to have lunch in the museum café, where he took his time enjoying a *salade niçoise*, good bread, and a glass of Muscadet. Of course, he could not leave without revisiting the Monets on the lower level. In one, swaying water weeds could be seen beneath the clear surface of a pond, which was also reflecting billowy clouds and blue sky. The illusion was dazzling and mysterious. Monet himself said that staring at it would drive you mad.

After leaving the museum, he did not return to the same metro station, but instead walked through a maze of quiet, leafy streets to the Avenue Mozart's station. One of his vague goals in life was to walk every street in Paris. When he grew foot weary on these jaunts, he would find a sidewalk café and order a Ricqlès over ice, a refreshing effervescent mint drink.

Sunday the weather was beautiful so he headed to the garden to read the newspaper. Children sailed toy boats in the basin, women sunbathed, and men played cards and *pétanque*. About 10:30, the bells of Saint-

Sulpice announced the final Mass, which would be followed by a brief but glorious organ recital. This temptation alone could wrench him from the delights of the garden. The organ of Saint-Sulpice was reputed to be the sweetest in all of France. Afterwards, lunch and a movie. That would be enough for the weekend. Tomorrow was going to be a big day.

PHILIPPE LACOUTURE WAS a *conservateur d'État* at the Institut des Hautes Études de l'Amérique Latine on Rue Saint-Guillaume. This institution had a growing library of 125,000 volumes, which concentrated on Latin American Studies. Three years before Michael had spent a day there thumbing through its catalog and consulting selected books in order to broaden his own knowledge of sources. He was mainly paying attention to European texts, but he couldn't help noticing English-language books too. Holdings in English were uneven, and he spotted some significant lacunae.

On his next trip to Paris, he went back to the library and asked to see the librarian responsible for collection development. A few minutes later a tall, thin man emerged from a door at the back of the reading

room and walked to the front desk. After they introduced themselves, Michael said:

"I'm a bookseller from California. The last time I
used this library, I noticed that you lacked an important
book on Mexico that I happen to own." He paused,
opened a manilla envelope, and removed a thick
volume. "It's Anita Brenner's *The Wind That Swept
Mexico*, published in 1943. I would like you to have it."

"Pardon, Monsieur, you wish to sell the book?"

"Not at all. I would like to give it to the library. To
perfect the collection, as you say in French."

Philippe set the book down on top of the desk and
leafed through its photographs of the Mexican Revolution. "How kind of you, Monsieur. This is a splendid
book. We accept it with pleasure. Thank you. May I
offer you a cup of coffee?"

Philippe's office displayed the reassuring clutter of a
scholar. He motioned Michael to have a seat, cleared a
space on the corner of the desk, and poured two cups
from a heated carafe.

"Where in California do you live?"

"Los Angeles."

"Ah, Los Angeles. Five years ago my family and I
flew to Los Angeles in order to begin a trip to the
Southwest. We rented a car and drove to Arizona and
New Mexico. Fabulous! The Grand Canyon, Monu-

ment Valley, the Hopi Pueblos, Santa Fe. Fabulous! We rode horses. We even grew to love the hot, spicy food."

"It is unique—and for me the most interesting part of our country. I'm glad to see that your library is collecting material on it."

"Why not? It belonged to Spain and Mexico for three centuries and in some respects still does. The book you gave us—is it the sort that you sell?"

"Yes. Mexico and the Southwest are two of my subjects."

"And would you, perhaps, be interested in looking for others that we need?"

"But of course."

It was agreed that Philippe would send a list of desiderata to which Michael could suggest additions. Quoting and ordering would be done by e-mail. So began a satisfying business relationship, with books crossing the Atlantic in a direction opposite from usual.

On the present occasion Philippe had asked Michael to show up a little before noon. After an effusive greeting, he put on his coat, and said, "No business in the library today. In fact, you're just in time for lunch." The restaurant was a few streets away, so they walked over. It was small and unremarkable from the outside, but refined and comfortable within. A burst of fresh flowers, a true zinc bar, a charming woman to greet them, Belle Epoque lighting, and at their table gleaming linen and beautiful tableware. Philippe was lean, but like most of his compatriots he loved the rituals of fine dining. They ordered *apéritifs*: a Lillet Blanc for Michael served with a few pistachios and a *fino* for Philippe served with olives. Both studied the menu, pausing often to talk.

"In the last shipment, I was thrilled to see Elsie Clews Parsons' *Taos Pueblo*—not the reprint, mind you, but the original 1936 edition. How do you do it? I know about the scandal her report caused when it was first published for revealing secrets such as the organization of the kivas. The tribe was outraged, and flogged or fined the informants who told Miss Parsons."

"Yes, one Indian warned that, if she came back to the pueblo to try to smooth things over, they would have to scalp her."

The waiter took their order, and a few minutes later brought out the entrées: a *salade de homard avec des tomates et haricots verts*, a lobster salad, for Michael and *girolles à la crème*, chanterelle mushrooms sautéed in butter and cream, for Philippe. To accompany these dishes they shared a half bottle of Meursault.

"So what's the picture like for French libraries? How are you doing?"

"My friend, do you hear a great sucking sound in

Paris? A deafening noise? It's the BNF, of course, the new national library. Every spare *centime* goes into fixing the design errors of this colossal institution. Our budgets are being squeezed dry. And this, unfortunately, means we are ordering less and less from our suppliers —including you, I'm sorry to say."

"I've started to notice. You turned down some very good books on the last list."

"It kills me, but I have no money. How is business at home?"

"In steady decline, due to an obsession with electronics and a conviction that the computer will replace the book. There is still money but it has been shifted to new interests. Worse, I've just lost my best customer, George Rosen, at the state university, a man you would love."

"French librarians are beginning to adore electronics too. It's becoming the way to get ahead in our profession. New libraries are called *mediathèques* not *bibliothèques*."

"But at least the French seem more balanced, and display some common sense. For example, the director of Lyon's great municipal library, Patrick Bazin, has stated that academic reading—what he calls 'reading from A to Z'—is over for most people. Mainly because of competition from other media. He asks, 'How do you read enormously, see lots of movies, and travel—all at the same time?' But this belief of his did not stop him from accepting a humongous donation of rare books from the Jesuits, the entire library of their château in Chantilly, about 500,000 volumes."

"Of course not. Bazin's no fool."

The waiter reappeared, and both looked up with delight as he presented their main courses: *fricassée de lapin, sauce au vin rouge*, savory stewed rabbit served with caramelized onions and a golden potato galette, for Michael and *canard aux pruneaux*, roast duck in a port and prune sauce served with root vegetables, for Philippe. A robust Côte Rôtie was the wine of choice.

For a few moments they just ate, sighing, tasting, inhaling truly good food.

Then Philippe looped back to something mentioned earlier: "It must be a blow to lose your best client."

"George? Yes, terrible—and not only because of the money. He's left town, the person I most enjoyed talking to. I think you would really like him—a book-man, a scholar-librarian, among the last of the breed in America. I often wished that the three of us could get together. In recent years, he would spend his vacations on archaeological digs in Central America. Said it was a great way to sweat off fat and get back in shape. After a year spent in the library he enjoyed swinging a pickax, as well as the more careful digging, brushing, measuring, and recording. Most of all he enjoyed the camaraderie of the expedition in the middle of a jungle: swapping stories, watching stars, speculating about the lives of the ancient dead they were uncovering."

"Why did he leave?"

"I don't know. A political disagreement."

"This is the kind of person they are getting rid of?"

Dessert was offered, and this wonderful meal required it. Michael ordered *sorbets aux trois parfums* and Philippe *nougatine glacée*, coffee to follow.

While they were waiting, Philippe leaned forward. "My friend, may I ask you a personal question?"

"Go on."

"I know that you are not married, but is there anyone special in your life?"

"Not currently."

"What a pity, I mean, that my daughters aren't older or I would introduce them to you."

It was dark outside and inside the room. Michael, lying face down on the bed, still wore his clothes from lunch.

He reached over to turn on the bedside lamp, and sat up. From his wallet he removed a folded slip of paper with a telephone number on it.

"Elise?"

"Yes."

"This is Michael."

She said nothing, then: "Why do you phone me again after such a long time?"

"Because I tried to stop doing this."

"So why don't you?"

"I tried."

"You want me to let you into my life again. How many times have I done that? If I was going with somebody, I said no, but if I was unattached, I said yes, come over. Well, I'm with a man now and we plan to marry."

"Then we need to see each other one more time."

"Why?"

"To conclude."

MICHAEL's last business appointment was with one of the great men of the trade. There were only a few of them. All were older men, heritors from their fathers of lore, acumen, contacts, and stock. The French word is *fonds*, which means collections, assets, capital. Their rich *fonds* remained fundamental for whole domains of scholarship, history, literature, philosophy, science, and art. Their bookshops, so deceptively restrained, often had back rooms extending through entire blocks in the oldest parts of Paris, down into basements and up into second stories. They were veritable treasuries. The ordinary book hunter never saw any of this, of course, was never permitted to step foot into the sanctum sanctorum of bibliographical greatness. These men testifed as expert witnesses in courts of law. The sales catalogues they issued possessed such authority and erudition that discerning collectors and librarians kept them for reference. A few would even be reprinted, deemed classic bibliographies. The finest books in the world passed through their hands. Indeed the French government, the Bibliothèque Nationale, and the Ministry of Culture kept a nervous watch on their most important offerings—unique manuscripts, maps, musical scores, and photographs—which might raise questions of cultural patrimony. Newspapers would ask: Will the government allow this French treasure to leave the country?

Monsieur Pierre Keller's receptionist immediately recognized Michael and warmly greeted him as he had been a longtime customer. She led him back through a vaulted room used for preparing shipments, then up a circular staircase to an office which was situated just above the shop. Tall windows on the street side let clear northern light enter this room of stunning contrasts. Generously proportioned, its stone walls were lined floor to ceiling with neatly shelved books of every size printed between the fifteenth and eighteenth centuries, all bound either in parchment or leather, some regally decorated with coats of arms stamped in gold. The open center of the room, however, was entirely modern. The curved desk, side chair, sofa, coffee table, and lamps were of Italian design, fashioned from Brazilian hardwoods, black leather, aquamarine glass, and steel. The variegated walls of ancient books, having become background, then resembled abstract paintings. The effect was brilliant.

Monsieur Keller rose from his desk and shook Michael's hand. He had some coffee ready, and sat down beside Michael on the sofa to share it. They chatted for a while, catching up on each other's lives. Then he grinned. "Let me show you what I've found." He went back to his desk to retrieved a small volume and a manilla file folder, which he placed in the middle of the coffee table. Again, he sat down next to Michael. With a small flourish, he opened the folder. It was an engraving of Gabriel Naudé, Cardinal Mazarin's librarian, done by Claude Mellan.

"In my entire career, I've never seen one for sale before. It came from the estate of a family which has unfortunately died out. One of countless odd little treasures they owned. We believe it was done about 1649."

"Extraordinary."

"I was tempted to keep it for myself, but I knew someone who would desire it even more."

"You honor me, Monsieur. I can't thank you enough."

"Of course, the price is dear. It has to be. I'm asking 12,000 euros."

Michael blanched. "I'm sure I will never see another again."

"No you won't."

Then they turned their attention to the little volume. It was Naudé's *Questio secunda iatrophilologica: an vita hominum hodié quàm olim brevior?* published in Caesenae in 1634. An essay which asks how man attains knowledge when life is so short. That is the question, Michael thought. He would need to get out his Latin grammar and dictionary to puzzle out this text. It too was very rare and priced at 1,500 euros.

THAT NIGHT IN HIS ROOM, seated at a small writing table, Michael studied the portrait. Naudé is looking to the left. He has an appealing face, with mustache and goatee, and fine, large eyes. His gaze is steady and contemplative. He is wearing a dark unadorned coat topped by a broad white collar, which looks like the dress of a priest—or a musketeer.

Then Michael remembered a portrait of another librarian and couldn't help smiling—this one by Giuseppe Arcimboldo. His subject, too, is turned to the left, and has a beard. But the rest of him is whimsically formed from a pile of books. It is an artistic joke—a composite head—enormously popular when painted in the mid-sixteenth century.

He saw the two faces side by side. Naudé was the consummate librarian, and so it was his fate to transmute into the books he had collected. They are what remains from a lifetime of largely anonymous work. Only an occasional reader or scholar awed by a magnificent collection will perceive a face behind it.

Because he believed in the preeminence of intellect, he was an elitist. It made no difference that he came from a modest family, or that he would live simply all his life. Ignoring family advice, he pursued medicine rather than theology. Philosophically he was a skeptic, yet he worked for Princes of the Church—Cardinals

Bagni, Barberini, Richelieu, and Mazarin—and died piously. He realized that only rich and powerful persons could have libraries. Reason enough to enter their service, and become an apologist for them. Although he despised the masses, he built a great public institution: the finest library in Europe and the first in France open to everyone. He also watched it destroyed and desperately attempted to save it. Near the end he would be brutally humiliated in court. "He who dreamed of saving others from oblivion," Sainte-Beuve said much later, "is most regrettably among those who are foundering in the great wreck."

WHEN MICHAEL STARTED COMING to Paris at age 20, he didn't know anyone. At first he didn't care since the city itself excited him. There was so much to take in that he didn't have time to brood. But eventually he wanted someone to talk to. He found French society extremely hard to penetrate. His conversations were limited to a few words with shopkeepers, waiters, and hotel clerks. His French wasn't good either. He was totally incompetent, linguistically, to flirt with a girl sitting on a park bench, even if that were his style. Girls were everywhere, but usually they were hanging out with their friends. Walking, talking, laughing, drinking, eating. Everyone having a good time, especially at the hour of the *apéritif*, when they left work or school to join their pals at a sidewalk café to have a drink. Unfortunately, these circles were closed. Gradually he realized that the French invest heavily in family and friends until there is nothing left over (attention, time, interest) for anyone else. If you're out-group, you essentially don't exist.

Not willing to give up, he thought he might stand a better chance if he improved his French. He enrolled in the École Antoine Rivarol de la Langue Française. Located near Père-Lachaise Cemetery, it was a well maintained three-story building, painted white with blue trim, which included a nice courtyard and a canteen. A prospective student could enroll for one week at a time, one month at a time, or continuously. It catered to tourists, foreign visitors, foreign workers, and expatriates. Classes were small, no more than eight, and were offered at all levels from beginning to advanced. The instructors were French, but everyone else in the building was from somewhere else.

The first thing Michael noticed was that women outnumbered men about four to one. In his own class of Intermediate French, students came from Colombia, Ecuador, Germany, Great Britain, South Korea, and the U.S. The instructor was friendly and kept things informal. He soon had them working together, drilling grammar and practicing mini-conversations, each day with a different partner. For once, awkwardness elicited aid, not scorn. The familiarity of the class carried over to the canteen, where on half-hour breaks it was easy to talk to classmates, albeit in broken French, as he declined to speak English. Most of them loved being in Paris and wanted to stay as long as possible. But there were so many difficulties: a visa about to expire, trying to get a work permit, finding a job, finding an apartment, maybe even a Frenchman! The girls would giggle when they said that. But they were all looking for a little romance and excitement. Meantime they worked as au pairs, yet often felt exploited by the sponsoring French family, beginning to feel like slaves. They loved to go out, but could hardly afford it. It was an old story. The wonderful desperation and exhilaration of youth in Paris.

Michael realized that he could graze in these pastures. He only needed to be a bit of a rogue. This thought buoyed him up, but did not put an end to his loneliness. It became an ache when he noticed that the German girl in class was looking at him intently. Strictly speaking she wasn't a girl. She was in her mid-twenties, a brunette, quietly attractive, and conservative in dress, yet anyone could see she had a nice figure. He asked her if she would like to have a cup of coffee after class, and when that went well to have dinner in a small bistro in the *quartier*. She lived with a family in the suburbs, tutoring the children in German, but she seriously hoped to get a job as a graphic designer. She had completed a two-year course in that subject at a technical institute in Germany.

At the bistro she looked lovely in candlelight and the food and wine were delicious. When they left, she walked close to him, even bumping against him, navigating the cobblestones. It was easy to put his arm around her as they walked. That felt so good. Then on a quiet side street, in the night shadow of a tree, they kissed. Desire in dreams is expressed with startling directness, and that is how it was from the first moment. Elise just leaned into him, kissing ardently. And inside Michael, a levee broke, his mind began roiling, in particular when he felt her breasts rubbing his chest. Hoarsely, he asked if she wanted to go to his room.

They made love with equal hunger from equal loneliness in a small hotel in the City of Paris. Michael found oblivion as he thrust into her over and over, and Elise found intense pleasure then contentment. Many demons were laid to rest. Afterwards she said that she felt safe with him—that she thought she knew him—

because of the class. Otherwise, she would be embarrassed by how fast it happened.

They became inseparable. Neither had much money, yet it didn't matter. Paris offered delights for all pocketbooks. Foremost its beauty. They walked and explored and laughed and ate in little places. Elise spoke excellent English, but she agreed that they should converse in French only, the bedroom being a good place to learn. They made amazing progress.

This could have gone on and on, and taken a natural course, except that one miserable day Michael ran completely out of money and knew he had to leave France.

HE WENT BACK TO L.A., got a job, enrolled in a graduate program in Romance Languages, and began scouting for rare books on the side. It turned out he had an aptitude for the last activity, thanks to a fine memory, a good education, and tenacity. He especially liked the idea of buying a book for $25, reading it, and then selling it for $50. And that was the wholesale price. If he became a dealer, he could sell it for $150. For an impecunious youth, the math proved irresistible.

Now, years later, he was on his way to see Elise. She
had asked him not to come to her apartment, but to
meet at a little café they both knew in a different
quartier. Greeting cautiously, they bussed each other on
the cheeks, his hands grasping her upper arms. She had
not put on an ounce of weight, adopting the way of
French women. They sat down in a booth and ordered
coffee. Her mauve scarf was artfully knotted over a
gray woolen pullover—the only color she chose to wear.
No lipstick. Darkened eyes betrayed a bad night.

"How's work? Are you still at that advertising
firm?"

"Yes, they put me in charge of a small design
group. I have my own office and an assistant."

"Good. Does your work appear in magazines?"

"No, we do catalogues and brochures. Slick and
colorful." She stopped.

"Listen," she said, "if you don't mind, I don't want
to catch up, with your life or mine. I came because I am
still a free woman, at least for a short while. And
because you are the person—the one person—I always
hope I will see again. What do you want to say to me?"

He took a moment.

"Elise, my feelings for you—I won't apologize for

them, but I will for wasting your time. At first I didn't want to settle down. Later I couldn't decide. Booksellers don't make good marriage material. We're lone wolves. We travel a lot. We work long hours. We're obsessed, and don't know when to quit looking, and for some books, never quit. I figured a marriage would break up."

"I loved you."

"I'm sorry."

"For a long time. What I wanted wasn't complicated."

"Except that I am. I was a fool."

"You are! And a coward too. You just couldn't take the leap. Anyway it's too late. The next time you come to Paris, I'll be married. Please, never phone me again."

3

When Michael returned to L.A., he was sullen. María noticed it right away, and thought that he had caught some disease on the airplane, perhaps the flu. She urged him to go home. He leafed through the mail that she had neatly organized, then agreed that maybe she was right. He left the office and did not return for the rest of the week. Only a long-scheduled appointment with his accountant brought him in the following Monday. The accountant was an older guy named Barney who always played the role of Dutch uncle to Michael's high flying ways, but on this occasion he read him the riot act. His business was on the verge of going down the drain. There was little in accounts receivable while accounts payable had burgeoned. He had been buying too many collections and too many pricey books. Did he have customers for them? Sales on the Internet had been fair and business with the French librarian good, but these were the sole life rafts keeping him afloat. Maybe he should consider closing his doors and getting a real job.

This put Michael in a truly dark mood, but it also spurred him to action. He began phoning librarians all over the country, offering them his choicest items, especially those just acquired in France. He sold a few, but it was tough going. Money seemed to be tight everywhere. His best prospect was with a steady customer and friend, a Latin American bibliographer at one of the Arizona universities. He offered her a remarkable group of pamphlets about the French intervention into Mexico, which took place from 1861 to 1867. A tragical farce on the French side, heroic nation building on the Mexican. The story of the brief reign of Maximilian and Carlotta, including uprisings and decisive battles, folly and duplicity, the Emperor's capture, trial, and execution by the forces of Benito Juárez, and Carlotta's final madness. Juicy stuff. More than 150 titles collected by an officer who served under Maximilian. Many were eyewitness accounts. Being pamphlets, their print runs, distribution, and life expectancy were predictably short, but these had remained undisturbed in the family library for over a century. After they found a home in a special collections department of a research library, many Ph.D. dissertations, articles, and books could be squeezed out of them.

The Arizona librarian was interested at once and asked him to hold the collection until she could see it. Luckily she would be in L.A. soon to attend a Southwest Region Library Network meeting. She would come by after it was over.

MICHAEL'S BUSINESS did not get walk-in trade. It was located in a business park and looked like a small warehouse. Indeed, two thirds of the space was dedicated to storing books. The other third consisted of a shipping and receiving area, an outer office with computers, copiers and files, a restroom, a food preparation nook, and his office. Carpeting, lighting, and artwork softened the industrial setting and created a pleasant ambiance.

His office was fairly large, because it included sufficient room to bring in collections that he was either cataloging or planning to show to clients. A long Tuscan trestle table divided the room into two spaces. On the side near the door there was a desk and leather couch, suitable for taking naps. On the other side, floor-to-ceiling wall shelving, as well as lower, double-sided bookcases, constructed in alder by a local craftsman. A spectacular serigraph by John Nieto called *Gray Wolf* hung behind the desk. Nearby an antique library cabinet with glass doors held his personal collection on Gabriel Naudé.

Since they seldom dealt directly with the public, Michael and María dressed casually. María would typically wear jeans and a blouse, or a sweatshirt when the weather turned cold. She was sensitive to the fact that they worked almost entirely alone, and while Michael was a wonderful boss who respected her, she didn't want to unnecessarily rile him up by wearing a tight sweater or a short skirt. She knew all about that. She was a twenty-four-year-old single mother with a seven-year-old girl. In high school, instead of studying, she had spent far too much time in the backseat of a car with her boyfriend. Despite the embarrassment of giving birth to a baby in her senior year, she had managed to graduate, thanks to her family. She had learned her lesson, but it was nonetheless difficult keeping men off her.

This was a good job for her. The hours were not rigid, so if the school phoned and said that her daughter was sick, she could take off early without recrimination. The job had also opened her eyes to a whole different world, way beyond her Mexican-American neighborhood. Who else had even heard of international bookselling? During her first week she was in awe, although she tried to hide it. Fortunately they traded with Mexico and conducted a lot of business in Spanish. This was her hook. When Michael was away she handled the phones as well as routine correspondence, whether in English or Spanish. Having learned to type in high school, she easily adapted to word processing. She packed and unpacked shipments, shelved books, and kept the place neat. And little by little she became curious about scholarship. The old leather-bound books with their beautiful title pages seemed wonderfully exotic, and she couldn't believe the prices people paid for them. It delighted her that she could read those written in Spanish, after adjusting to the funny typography. Michael never objected to her doing a little reading on the job, and gradually she began reading books of her own while eating lunch and before going to sleep at night. Finally, she made a big decision: to go back to school at Los Angeles City College, which she could do in the evening if her mother babysat.

For his part, Michael was quite satisfied. María didn't know a thing when she started but she quickly caught on. He noticed too that she instinctively handled books with respect and care, something that many dunces, even the educated kind, never understand. When business was down, her humor, sarcasm, and loyalty sustained him, and when it was up, she preened with enthusiasm. The only potential problem with María was that she was very nice to look at—and to smell fresh from a shower. He had to caution himself about that.

AFTER SHE FELT MORE secure in her position, María asked Michael where he learned Spanish. This had impressed her. She discussed it with her mother. Then she bragged to her friends that she was working for an Anglo who spoke the language of la Raza better than they could.

"Half the people in this city speak Spanish. Why shouldn't I?"

"No one else feels that way."

He laughed. "Booksellers do what they want."

"Are you part Spanish?"

"No."

"French?"

"Not a drop."

"Then how come you bothered?"

"I could say 'to see things from a different angle,' but that's more an effect than a cause. Polyglot envy. To be cool. To decipher the exotic, which the French and Mexicans were for me in the beginning."

Her brown eyes widened. She considered stopping right there to think about what he had said, but couldn't. "In Mexico, do they take you for a Mexican?"

"Sometimes. Don't you think I look like one?"

"No."

"You're hurting my feelings."

Getting this much out of him pleased her. "How did you become a bookseller, I mean of Spanish books?"

"Almost by accident. Brawn not brains. I started out as a pack animal. Not a mule, but definitely a burro. There was this old curmudgeon named Ed Stearns, who had a shop on Melrose Avenue. Today he wouldn't be able to afford the location, were he still alive. He specialized in Western Americana and Mexico. I scouted for him. Whenever I came by he seemed to brighten, not because of the books I had found, but because, as often as not, crates and cartons were piled at the door needing to be moved inside, unpacked, and shelved. I didn't mind helping him, and I made him pay by asking questions. It was hard to tell whether he really didn't like answering or only pretended, but he forked over anyway. I learned a lot about the business from him.

"One day, out of the blue, he asked me if I wanted to take a trip to Mexico. Said he was getting too old to haul around books. Needed a helper. He would pay my way down plus a little spending money. I said sure. He set the date and told me to bring no more than one small suitcase.

"On the day of departure the shop was closed, but he was inside waiting for me. A gigantic suitcase was spread open on the floor, which he was filling with wrapping paper, twine, tape, scissors, and shipping labels. He told me to carry it out to the car. I expected we would head to the airport, but this guy got on the freeway going the opposite direction, to San Bernardino. Turned out he hated to fly. We were going to take the train, from Mexicali to Mexico City. Some other time I'll tell you about the trip down—a real eye opener—which took three days."

"Why not now?"

"Because if I start talking about Mexico, I'll embark on an infinite regress."

"A what?"

"A long story. We wouldn't get any work done. Anyway, in the capital we stayed in a hotel that catered to traveling salesmen."

"I know the kind: *bueno, bonito, y barato*."

"Not too *bonito*. After we settled in, Ed unfolded a large map of the city to plot an itinerary. Then he phoned a taxi driver he knew to reserve his services for the whole week. I do the same thing now. It's convenient, and a way of avoiding rogue drivers in look-alike cabs who will rob you. The next day, our first stop was the *Excélsior* newspaper office, where Ed placed a want ad offering to buy old and unusual books pertaining to Mexican history. Said he was weary of making the rounds and wanted to see if stuff would come to us. But we did make the rounds, starting with great rare book dealers like Porrúa Hermanos and Antigua Librería Robredo—a day each—then on to smaller shops, and finally to the secondhand book stalls of the sprawling Lagunilla flea market. His Spanish was good, and it was fascinating to see his personality change when he was in these places. He smiled, shook hands, gave them his calling card, and bantered as though he were a friendly man. Perhaps he *was* in Mexico. Ed liked the country, and maintained that without courtesy, respect, and a total disregard for time, you got nowhere with Mexicans."

"I like this man."

"*Cuidado*. If he had heard that, the next thing you

know his hand would be on your knee. Especially *your* knee."

"I still like him."

"Sorry, he's dead. Anyway, whenever we returned to our hotel room, the phone would be ringing. Because of the ad. Some callers were cautious, some crafty, some excited. Screening them was difficult. We gave most an appointment, asking them to bring whatever they were selling. About four-fifths of it was worthless thrift shop material. But the final fifth was interesting. Honestly, we had no idea where it came from. We were always told it was *en la familia*, something a grandparent had saved. I remember blowing dust off a set of account books and ledgers from the Hacienda San Diego in the state of Chihuahua, which belonged to the powerful Terrazas family. I remember an old cookbook, *Manual del cocinero y cocinera* (1849), which Ed sold to a chef. And most of all I remember a young man who brought in five shoe boxes full of photographs of the Mexican Revolution, shot by his grandfather. Remarkably many of these photos were taken in the midst of great battles, like Torreón and Zacatecas, not just skirmishes within the capital. Unposed scenes of raw action were highly unusual. You can imagine the danger and difficulty of recording it.

"The old man said he wanted them, would buy

them, provided the seller could get them to Los Angeles. The cost of travel would be added to the price. They bargained quietly, seriously, for a long time, and shook on it. He took a chance and paid twenty percent in earnest right then—cash of course."

"Did they arrive?"

"Oh, yes. *Intacto*. Looking back I know it was a lucky trip—even though I did get sick."

"*¿Turista?*"

"The worst ever."

LATER MICHAEL WAS STILL THINKING about their conversation. He liked his way of life. True, he had been in some tight spots, at the mercy of a corrupt cop or a thug, but he had always managed to talk or bribe his way out. A cost of doing business, unfortunately not tax deductible. Only one thing scared him: dying alone in a hotel room. Whenever he became seriously ill on a trip—from food poisoning, amoebic dysentery, the flu, blinding migraines—dread enshrouded him. He realized that this fear was irrational, because if he died at home, in his own bed, he would most likely be alone. Both his parents were dead, he was their only child, he had no wife. They had done a good job of preparing

him to be on his own. An engineer married to an econ-
omist. Both valued competence. They would cheerfully
answer all his questions and show him exactly how to
do things, but they expected to never be asked the same
question twice. That would cause a sigh, a sad look, a
frown. Not that they didn't love him. They never
stinted in cultivating his mind. Conversations at the
dinner table were spirited. But he was expected to live
up to family standards. Too bad the family was going to
end with him.

DURING THE LULL Michael and María worked on
creating and inputting records of their entire inventory,
so that they would display on their website as well as on
the big search engines of out-of-print book services, like
Alibris and Abebooks. Only about half of the inventory
had been previously listed. Still excluded were the
collections that Michael did not want to break up.
María could do this faster than Michael, but she had to
wait on him to price the books.

The Internet was simultaneously the best and worst
thing that had happened to antiquarian bookselling.
On the one hand it potentially exposed a dealer's stock
to the entire world. A book purchased in Mexico City

and brought to Los Angeles, for example, when listed online, might be resold to a customer in Guadalajara— or Boston or Madrid. On the other hand, internet selling was faceless and anonymous. There was no opportunity for a rapport to develop between the bookseller and the book collector, and to learn of the latter's interests. The days when antiquarian booksellers had long-standing relationships with libraries, acting as both scouts and filters, had all but disappeared. Yet this was how most great libraries originally built their collections, collections they are so proud of now, which can no longer be replicated, and which lure top scholars.

THE DAY of Irena Kushner's visit finally arrived. She drove over in a rental car after the library network meeting concluded, arriving about 4 PM. She had made arrangements to fly back to Arizona the next day. It was a happy reunion as they had known each other for a long time, first meeting at the annual Seminar on the Acquisition of Latin American Library Materials and then bumping into each other at the Guadalajara Book Fair. Michael introduced Irena to María, who soon left to pick up her daughter at school.

Irena descended from an uprooted family of

Russian intellectuals. Medical doctors, architects, teachers. They were outspoken liberals, who luckily had an instinct for knowing when to flee. From Saint Petersburg to Berlin to Santiago to San Francisco. One dislocation each generation. Irena had been an assistant professor of literature at the Universidad de Chile when Allende was overthrown and assassinated. She was a partisan. One night she heard a thud on her door, which turned out to be the corpse of a colleague. The next night she was gone. Several months later she surfaced in the U.S., where she stayed with friends. Through the influence of one, she was able to land a university job cataloging Spanish books in the library. It was lowly work after being a professor, but she found that she didn't mind and gradually moved up the ladder.

A sample of the French Intervention pamphlets were spread out on the Tuscan table. The rest were in a nearby bookcase. Irena began poring over them, reading the title pages aloud with a slight slavic accent:

"Miguel García Vargas, *Intervención francesa en la República de México: opúsculo.* 1863.

"*Que ferons-nous à Mexico?* 1863.

"Rafael Martínez de la Torre, *Carta a Mr. Victor Hugo*. 1867.

"Cyprien Millot, *Question mexicaine l'empereur est mort!* 1867."

"There are 103 titles in French and 48 in Spanish, all published in the nineteenth century. The collector died in 1898. Quite a number are exceedingly rare and are held by only one or two libraries. The French group constitutes a very high percent of what was published on the subject in that language during the period."

"*C'est incroyable!* How on earth did you find it?"

"I'm one of the few U.S. dealers who pounds the pavement in France looking for Latin Americana. So they remember me. I received a tip from a dealer who had no interest in it but who knew its value. He was negotiating with the family for other stuff in their library, and he brought me in to sweeten the deal."

"I think I will need to stay here all night to absorb this—but may I look around? This is my first time in your shop."

Michael escorted her with pleasure to the back room which housed his stock. She browsed for a half hour and picked out a few items, then returned to the office. She paused in front of the case holding Naudé.

"Are these for sale too?"

"No, that's my collection—still incomplete. I don't know a library that's worthy of it."

"Ooh la la, we must talk."

"Good. Would you like to grab some dinner? I know a nice Lebanese restaurant not far from here."

FORTY-FIVE MINUTES later they were comfortably seated before plates of hummus, baba ghanoush, lamb stew with tomatoes and okra, and a bottle of Brouilly. Both loved this kind of food and used pita bread more than forks to scoop up mouthfuls dripping with sauce.

"So tell me about Naudé. All I know is that he was a French librarian. Why do you find him so interesting?"

"When I became a bookseller and started selling to libraries, I read a history of the institution and found out that Gabriel Naudé more than anyone else invented research librarianship. He provided the theory and then set an example. His *Advis pour dresser une bibliothèque*, published in 1627, was the first comprehensive treatise about forming a universal and encyclopedic library."

Michael took a sip of wine. "Except for its anti-quated diction, you might not know when it was written. Its guidelines for developing a collection are—I can only describe them as breathtaking, in their sweep, tolerance, and rigor. This, at a time when books were still chained to shelves in most libraries, and heretical and prohibited books were kept in locked cases. You know, the French like to put theory first. They're all Cartesians. So Naudé had his theory. Fifteen years later, working for Cardinal Mazarin, he applied it, creating the finest library in Europe. Best of all, he opened it to the public."

"Bravo." Irena gestured for him to keep going.

"I suppose the second reason I like to collect Naudé is the sheer difficulty of doing so. His books were printed more than 350 years ago. They had short print runs. In fact, the original edition of *Considérations politiques sur les coups d'état*—because of its controversial content—he allowed to be published in only twelve copies. Imagine finding one. In short, he tests my skills."

"And your bank account! You're definitely a high maintenance man," she said smiling. "Now I know why your prices are so high."

"Irena, you're a friend, I would love to give you a really good deal on the French pamphlets, but I can't. Let me be honest, right now I have a cash flow problem and need money. All regular stock is on sale, but not this collection. It's quite special: important subject, remarkably complete, in beautiful condition, and loaded with rarities. It's a humdinger, definitely salable, the best stuff always is. So, regretfully, I must stick it to you."

"Are you?" she said, again smiling, looking straight at him. "How much?"

"$45,000."

"No way."

"In this case, the sum is greater than its parts."

"$40,000."

"Deal."

She laughed. "Well, let's hope I can swing it. I'll talk to the Head of Special Collections. Maybe we can split costs. Or, if necessary, I'll go to the Library Director. Given the University's interest in Mexico, it's a perfect collection."

"Exactly. Everybody's going to like it, including the local newspaper." Michael waived the waitress over and ordered some *baklava* and two Turkish coffees.

"Thank God for Latin Americanists! You're about the only group of librarians still ready and willing to buy books, including old books. You're acquisitive. You build collections the old-fashioned way. *Con entusiasmo.*"

"Yes, we frustrate the powers-that-be, but at present they can't do much about it, except cut our budgets and that risks faculty ire. Universities with area studies programs must collect what's out there, and in third world countries it's overwhelmingly printed material. We're expected, of course, to subscribe to all relevant databases, but luckily they're cheaper and less numerous in our field. Of course we don't dare put it that way when speaking out loud. To retain status we must appear as up to date and technologically obsessed as our colleagues."

THEY WENT BACK to the office, both in a good mood. Michael asked Irena if she would like a *digestif*. He produced a bottle of fine tequila, Don Julio Añejo, and two small snifters.

"That would be perfect," she said settling into the couch. "Is that your totem?" she asked, pointing to the serigraph of the wolf.

"No, no, it's just a good piece, visually exciting. The artist painted the energy of the animal, the auras and forces. It's similar to the brilliant patterns of scientific imaging."

"I think it looks just like you."

He handed her a glass and sank into the couch. "*¡Salud!*" They both sipped the liquor looking at each other, then she moved toward him and he kissed her. When he broke off she put her hand on the back of his neck and kissed him back, exploring his lips. Thus began an almost silent but fervent inquiry wherein both answered questions that they had formed about the other, questions that had occurred over the years as they met at conferences and watched each other across crowded, noisy receptions. Distance permitted wonder. Now he unbuttoned the top of her dress, slipped it off her shoulders, unhooked her bra, and then, yes, he knew. He cupped both her breasts, in awe at what a gift a woman is. Likewise Irena had her curiosities, which she took her time finding and uncovering and touching. Their last question was answered in concert when both exploded.

"Are you always like that?"

"I was trying to reach China."

"Did you get there?"

"Yeah."

IRENA DEPARTED A LITTLE BEFORE DAWN. She kissed him sweetly. "Honestly, I have long wanted to do this, but still I surprise myself by what I am capable of. I'm married, you know."

"Uh-huh."

"Happily married."

MICHAEL DIDN'T COME in until 1:00 PM the next day. María raised her eyebrows and studied him quizzically but couldn't hold back a grin. "You must have been working real late, Boss."

He didn't say anything, just smiled, and kept walking.

"I straightened up your office a little bit, and opened the windows. To air it out."

4

Although the sale of the French pamphlets brought a temporary financial reprieve, business was still down. Michael didn't understand what was going on. When he dropped into his local Barnes & Noble bookstore, it was loaded with people, enjoying the ambiance, drinking coffee and eating pastries, looking at magazines, and happily browsing row upon row of books. Long lines formed at the cash registers, and often enough he saw customers with a stack of books under their arm, which would cost a goodly sum. Amazon.com was flourishing, delivering packages everywhere, to remote Montana ranches or small Southern towns. Yet libraries had drastically cut back on the purchase of books—at least the kind he sold. He had been told that they relied on approval plans and data dumps which brought in new publications—mostly e-books—more or less automatically. That seemed to satisfy them. What annoyed him the most was his inability to purchase new stock during this period of stagnation. Business was so slow he was considering substitute teaching just to pay a few bills. Either that or pizza delivery.

One gloomy morning as he arrived at work, María announced that he had just missed a phone call from a librarian at the state university, a Ms. Elizabeth Wyatt. "Here's her number."

"The reason I phoned," he learned a few minutes later, "is that we might after all be interested in acquiring that collection you mentioned on French scientists and scholars in Latin America. Does that surprise you? I hope it does. I was wondering if I could make an appointment to see it."

A few days later she was striding around his office looking at everything and openly admiring the furnishings. She had not expected so much art in a place of business, she said. Finally she sat down on the couch exactly where Irena had lain. But Elizabeth was a different sort of woman: striking, well dressed, exuding ambition.

The French scientist collection was so large he had to store it in the back room with regular stock. That part of the building had no heating. Elizabeth walked along in high heels scanning several ranges while Michael followed, explaining the unusual nature of the collection and its potential value to scholars.

At the last shelf she turned to face him. "Yes, it's impressive. Grand. I think we definitely may want it. Can we go back to your office where it's warmer to discuss terms?"

"Of course."

It turned out that something big was brewing at the State U. They had been cultivating a donor, a CEO of an aircraft factory named Jack Carter, who was prepared to give them twenty-five million dollars towards the construction of a new undergraduate library, which would be state of the art—in other words, entirely electronic. Details were being worked out. It was imperative that the public announcement be a grabber. The publicity departments of the aircraft factory and the university were kicking around ideas for photo-ops and a human interest story, and they rejected the idea of the donor, the university president, and the library director shaking hands beside a boxy computer terminal—or anything like that—as just too boring. Instead they pictured these men standing in front of an opulent collection of rare books—a personal collection of the donor's that he was also giving to the university as a link between the past and the future, a bridge, an enduring symbol. That's where Michael came in. He had a beaut ready to go. Elizabeth would have the Head of Special Collections come by to render an expert second opinion, but she thought there would be no problem. How much did he want?

A quarter of a million.

Fine.

~

THIS CONVERSATION both intoxicated and unnerved him. The money was the answer to his prayers but it irked him that the books were desired only as eye candy. He would be handing them over to barbarians. Then he quickly reconsidered, remembering that he had formed the collection at the behest of George. It had always been intended for this library.

In the coming weeks, Michael and Elizabeth saw a lot of each other. She asked him to write up a complete description of the collection for background and publicity. Also to pick out high spots for a special exhibit and to write the legends. She showed him a draft of the reception program, a lavish, illustrated booklet, which would be printed on heavy paper.

They got along well together. It was obvious that

Michael's stock had risen. Elizabeth was impressed by his competence and professionalism, his writing style and erudition, and not least his looks.

The reception was a sumptuous affair, of a quality rarely seen anymore on public university campuses. It was held in the cavernous lobby of the main library, which had been closed early for the event. A string quartet played as visitors entered. Library staff members and university development officers rushed out to greet them and point the way to exhibits and refreshments. There was a scale model of the proposed building and a series of architectural renderings of its exterior and interior. The most spectacular of the rare books from the donated collection were also on display in a row of locked glass cases. Many had beautiful plates and typography, and did not disappoint. Uniformed waiters and waitresses swirled around the floor, serving excellent chardonnay and merlot as well as exceptional hors d'oeuvres to a crowd of well-dressed community and business leaders, university administrators, professors, spouses, and a few students. Michael saw Elizabeth chatting with the donor and his wife, the University President, the Provost, and the Library Director. She was radiant wearing an expensive dress that subtly amplified her beauty.

After a period of socializing, the crowd was called

to order, asked to take seats, and speeches began. It was the customary laudatory and academic fare, laced with superlatives and hyperbole. The President called the donor a statesman of business, a citizen scholar, and a visionary. The architect, trying to be funny, promised that the only paper to be found in the new library would be in printers and toilet stalls. For Michael, the best line came from the donor himself who said: "Frankly it's harder for me to give up my beloved book collection that I have spent so many years with than the twenty-five million. But I know both will be in good hands."

5

A month later Michael phoned Elizabeth to say hello. She was still floating from the effects of the big event. The Director wanted her to take over fundraising for the library and was creating a new position for that purpose at the Assistant Director level. She would also continue as Digital Resources Librarian and play a big role in formulating collection development policy. George's old position as bibliographer would be advertised, so she would be giving up those duties. Then she asked him what he was doing.

He told her he was going on an extended buying trip in Mexico—about a month—and when that was over he planned to take a few days off, a little vacation, in the old tropical beach town of Zihuatanejo. "I was wondering if you would like to join me there? It's a beautiful spot."

This caught her by surprise, and for a moment she said nothing. "But we haven't gone out, we haven't dated."

"That's true, but we certainly know each other. I was planning to reserve separate rooms, if you accepted."

A bit flustered, she said she would phone him back. It was too much to deal with at work.

FIVE WEEKS later he was waiting for her plane to arrive at a small airport about ten miles south of Zihuatanejo, a town on Mexico's Pacific coast about 1,600 miles south of the border. The airstrip was located parallel to the beach amidst palm and mango trees and pretty estuaries fed by rivulets descending from the foothills. Since it was late November, the air was balmy, the sunshine delightful. The airport could accommodate smaller commercial jets, and Elizabeth arrived on the 4:15 PM Alaska flight from Los Angeles. As soon as she had cleared customs, Michael greeted her with a quick hug and a warm *"bienvenida,"* gathered her bags, and led her to a waiting taxi.

The windows of the cab were rolled down, and the ride into town was breezy and fun. Alongside the road grass grew knee high, and citrus, date palm, and mango plantations extended to the foothills. The cab sped past occasional homes with tile roofs, whitewashed walls, and pretty verandas bursting with bougainvillea. As they neared town, housing became denser and climbed hillsides, but the land remained green and tropical. The taxi skirted most of the town, which is at one end of a lovely bay, and proceeded up a road cut out of the steep hillside. The beaches below displayed fine clean sand, gentle waves, and abundant tropical vegetation. Here and there small European-style hotels were embedded into the hillsides, and it was to one of these that the taxi brought them. Their hotel, like the others, offered the luxury of silence and isolation. There were neither TVs nor telephones. Instead, the rooms were elegant in their simplicity: whitewashed walls, saltillo tile floor, colorful fabrics and bathroom tiles, windows open to the sea breeze, billowing drapes, a shaded balcony with hammocks, flowering vines, and a view of the sea.

They were led to rooms that were side by side. He told her that she wouldn't truly have arrived in Zihu-atanejo until she felt the water, and he proposed that they go for a swim right away, as soon as she had a chance to unpack and get settled. She told him to knock on her door in about an hour.

When she emerged, wearing a two-piece bathing suit, he experienced a slight shock of seeing her in a whole new aspect. He tried not to stare at her body and merely said, "You look great." He led her down the serpentine walkway of the hill to the beach. The sun was low on the horizon, a few minutes away from setting. It lit up the bay splendidly. They set their towels down and went straight into the water, which was not at all cold, the virtue of tropical waters. Indeed, after the hassle of a day of flying, for Elizabeth the water felt utterly refreshing. As she began to swim and use her muscles, the stress and tension and fatigue of city life simply rippled off her.

An hour of swimming made them hungry. Michael suggested that they eat in one of the thatched-roofed restaurants down the beach. They found one with tables planted in the sand, and ordered *dorado a la parrilla*, *arroz*, *y calabacitas*, grilled mahi mahi, rice cooked with a little fresh corn and peppers, and tender green squash sautéed with onions —accompanied by limes, salsa, tortillas, and washed down with cold bottles of Pacifico beer. Nothing could be better and nothing else was needed. In darkness they made their way back to the hotel. Elizabeth felt blissfully tired and just wanted to sleep, so they said goodnight.

The next day he rapped on her door, inviting her for a morning swim. She said to come back in a half hour. Still sleepy, she followed him down the hillside, but once again the air temperature and water temperature were refreshing, neither cold nor hot. For an hour or so they simply enjoyed moving their bodies through the clear water, turning and rolling and kicking, or floating on their backs looking at the cloudless sky, noticing bobbing butterflies and gliding birds, or resting in shallow water with their feet planted in the sand, looking back at the hillside, enjoying a panorama of tropical vegetation and striking architecture, the small hotels and exotic houses of wealthy Mexicans.

With appetites roaring they found another open-air restaurant on the beach and had their first Mexican breakfast together, arguably the best meal of the day: a platter of fresh sliced fruit drizzled with lime juice, *café con leche*, a choice of eggs (*huevos rancheros* or *huevos con chorizo*) served with refried beans, a sprinkle of *queso cotija*, thinly sliced fried potatoes, corn tortillas, salsa, and to finish, a piece of *pan dulce*. A wonderful breakfast that completely eliminated the need to have lunch.

The rest of the day they lay on lounges under the trees, talking and reading and dozing. Above them in the branches were many birds. The most amusing was an intelligent and noisy grackle, who liked to swoop down, land nearby, and walk around them in the sand. His color, a lustrous midnight-blue, enchanted Elizabeth. Continuing to peer into the tree canopy, she saw orchids, vines, even an iguana.

When they needed to cool off, they went into the water. They began to play, and inevitably touched as they cavorted. The water made so much possible. Feeling Elizabeth's breasts and legs repeatedly brush him, Michael finally put his hand around her waist and pulled, bringing her in full against his chest. They kissed, and they remained in each other's arms. In wet bathing suits neither could disguise how they felt. Her nipples grew erect and the front of his trunks bulged.

"Would you like to go back to the room?"

"I think so."

When they entered he took her hand and led her to the bed. She lay back, he settled beside her, and they began to kiss and caress, soon losing restraint. He rolled away so they could peel off their bathing suits, then rolled back on top of her as she spread her thighs, drawing them up to cradle him. She was very moist, so he entered easily, as though submerging into a pool of burning water. Once inside he was on his way again.

To be so purely desired—and taken—moved her.

When it was over both lay on their backs panting, watching the ceiling fan, feeling weightless. His loins were tingling, the after effect of a prodigious ejaculation.

"I can see why the Latin Americans won't give up their siestas," she said turning over to doze for a while.

THAT NIGHT they went into town and dined at a restaurant known for its fine grilled meats and better-than-average Mexican wines. As they were devouring the food, Elizabeth asked Michael to tell her a war story.

He laughed. "I'm a noncombatant."

"Oh, come on."

"Okay, provided it's not self-incriminating. I'll tell one about an earlier era of the trade when smuggling was more colorful."

"You mean people bother to smuggle books?"

"Absolutely—when they've been stolen from archives or churches, or when the stuff is politically sensitive. It's still done. There are laws intended to stop it, to protect cultural patrimony. But even a person of great rectitude must occasionally wonder at the ironies of history and circumstance. For example, there is no question that many highly important documents found in the collections of American and European research libraries would no longer exist had not they been stolen and transported to a safer place. Warfare, neglect, moisture, rats, or fire would have consumed them in their homeland. Or deliberate destruction—by police and censors. The literary papers of a novelist who is out of favor with a regime, the minutes of the Communist Party clandestinely struggling against a military dictatorship, the photos of death squad victims—these have to be smuggled out to survive. That is the argument on one side. On the other, on the side of the people who have been robbed, it is an expropriation of their history, of their culture, by foreigners.

"I suppose I'm not so particular now. I was once offered a group of prime colonial documents. Unfortunately the seller was unable to explain their provenance. I suspected that they were hot, so I shied away from them. I didn't want to have anything to do with the looting of national treasure. However, a year later a great American university purchased the same collection for a large sum from one of my rivals. They announced it as a major advance for scholarship, and the bookseller's reputation soared, even though people in the know shook their heads at the deal.

"Well, in the old days, the reasons for smuggling

were much the same—greed being uppermost—but the means different. If the documents were valuable, secure transport was imperative. So picture a small, traveling Mexican circus—this takes place in the 1930s—which passes back and forth across the border, playing in dusty towns, entertaining people with its bearded lady and midgets and clowns, and thrilling them with the trapeze artists and a lion tamer. The lion was an old one, but still appeared ferocious, and his was the big act the people waited for. When it was over he was led back to his wagon, a large cage on wheels, and fed a haunch of raw meat. No one dared come too near this beast or stick their hands through the bars—including border inspectors. They loved seeing this animal too, and he always caused a commotion whenever the troupe arrived at an inspection station. The border guards would look over the circus pretty carefully but always waved it through. No important contraband was ever discovered, for of course it was safely located under the feet of the lion, beneath the planks of the cage, in a hidden compartment. Quite a number of extraordinary Mexican manuscripts and documents, which are now among the glories of North American research libraries, came across this way."

"Do we have any in our library?"

"Undoubtedly."

"Hmm. Do you know which ones?

"No."

"Come on."

"No, I can't say."

"Hmm. So how are books smuggled today?"

"Sorry, that's a trade secret."

After they left the restaurant they spent a couple of hours pleasantly wandering around the streets, looking into shop windows, stopping for an ice cream, finally ending up where everybody does at the little plaza beside the municipal hall, where local basketball teams play during the cool of the evening. They watched for a while, then took a taxi back to the hotel. They had difficulty keeping their hands off each other. That night she moved into his room.

WHEN HE OPENED his eyes the following morning he saw her propped on an elbow looking at him.

"Stay still, I'm looking. This is an inspection." Apparently satisfied, she placed her hand on his cock, gently rubbing and kneading until it surged. She bent over and kissed the glans ardently but quickly broke away and sat up on her knees, then climbed on top of him. She was smiling and her breasts loomed and bobbed as she reached behind to position him just right. "I read in a tourist pamphlet yesterday that the name 'Zihuatanejo' comes from an old Tarascan Indian word meaning 'place ruled by women.' I like that—and I think it's time you learn what it means." She lowered her hips in a delicious arc. "I think, Mr. Self-Sufficient, that you need to be taught a good lesson."

The rest of the week went much the same, either one or the other on top—or in some other interesting position. When they flew back to Los Angeles, landing in wind and rain, they were very tight together. During their holiday, neither had spoken much about their jobs. Elizabeth mentioned once that men thought she was overly ambitious.

6

Back in the office Michael learned that sales continued to be slow, but this didn't dampen his good mood. Bills had been paid, with enough money left to tide them over for a while. He was careful about purchases, and bargained hard for the lowest prices. He spent a lot of time on the phone trying to find new customers, and a lot of time trying to think up some new angle, some hot subject, some market niche he could fill to reposition or expand his business. Seeing Elizabeth regularly, of course, helped. They were at the point in their relationship when both were thinking about the longer term. They were falling for each other. The only nagging area of concern was personal philosophy—or was it professional philosophy?—which they continued to skirt.

Bookseller and librarian. Why was their case like a Democrat and a Republican, or a Catholic and a Protestant, contemplating marriage? Asking "Will it work?"

WHEN ELIZABETH PHONED she was excited. "A project I proposed has been approved. Something big. We're going to digitize the Carter rare book collection, French Scientists and Savants in Latin America. Mr. Carter loves the idea and will underwrite it. The Director is thrilled."

"What?"

"Isn't it beautiful?"

"Why would you want to do such a thing?"

"Well, of course, to save these books. To revalue them, to resuscitate them, to disseminate them around the world, and save them from extinction. It's their only chance."

"So you intend to make electronic copies. What about the originals?"

"We will put them into cold storage, into the dark archive."

"The what? But this means no one will ever read them."

"On the contrary, it means everyone can read them, not just a few privileged scholars."

"No, I think it means no one will read them. The paradox of the Digital Age is that more books than ever are accessible, but reading has tanked. Why don't you simply return the books, after digitization, to Special Collections?"

"Well, because of technical issues. As you know, many of these books are fragile. Even using the most advanced copy equipment, the process does result in some wear and tear. Especially if we keep to a production schedule. In some cases, it may be necessary to disbind volumes, which were bound too tightly in the first place, in order to lay the pages flat to get the best possible reproduction. Unfortunately, our budget won't allow us to bring them back to their original physical condition, which isn't possible anyway. Let's say near original condition. Rare book conservation is horrifically expensive. It has to be done in labs, by experts. So we plan to tie the binding to its text block with string, and place it in storage, where cool temperature, perfect humidity, and darkness will preserve it better than ever."

"Elizabeth, this would be a disaster, a crime. Don't do it. Don't even think of doing it."

"But we are! Michael, you truly disappoint me. I

thought you would be pleased by my news. Instead, you're ranting."

As soon as he hung up the phone, he tore into the outer office to tell María. She listened intently, and winced several times, finally crying out: "They plan to destroy these books? In order to save them? It's like Vietnam. Who told you this?"

"Elizabeth."

"Isn't she your, uh, new girlfriend?"

"Yeah."

"I find that odd."

"No, no, it's not personal. I don't take it that way. It's a professional disagreement."

"You think like a gringo, Boss."

MICHAEL WAS STILL HAVING trouble registering what Elizabeth had said. He remembered a newspaper article about a Japanese art collector, fabulously wealthy, who had acquired a Van Gogh at auction. He keeps it at home, to himself, and has left instructions, when he dies, to have it destroyed. He has a right to do this, he says, because he owns it. In truth, there are many reproductions of this painting in books. Does that make any difference? Could they substitute for the original? Hardly.

Michael and Elizabeth had agreed to meet to talk some more. This was the weirdest part. Just a few nights ago they had been joyously making love in her apartment after attending a Cuban jazz concert. Now they were "agreeing to meet" like an estranged couple.

At a coffee shop near the university they found a booth toward the back. Both felt awkward. He stirred his coffee for a while before beginning.

"This disagreement is turning us upside down. It's absurd. I've been racking my brains to find another way.

"You think I've been enjoying it?"

"Of course not. Look, you have a very generous donor, someone who wants to make a difference. There are other worthwhile things he could spend his money on."

"Obviously."

"No, I mean for the library. You could, for example, encourage him to support other collecting ventures. Libraries everywhere are stretched thin and are acquiring a decreasing amount of the total publishing output. They are neglecting all kinds of subjects and areas of the world. There are collections in private hands going a-begging, especially those tracking the avant-garde. Right now there is an opportunity to quietly corner the market in subject after subject that will be of interest to future scholars. You could transform your library into a great center of research, following the example of Harry Ransom at the University of Texas at Austin. It only requires vision —and money. Your donor would be remembered and honored far into the future if he did this."

"It won't fly. The future is digital not print."

"But people who read—who read books—aren't clamoring for a change. They learned to love reading in the warmth of their mother's lap. Once started, they never stopped, regardless of whether the words were on a page or on a screen. Many are trying out the new electronic devices, and there's been a surge in the sale of e-books. Meanwhile, the kids are using the same devices to play video games, polish their Facebook profile, watch TV, and listen to music. Anything but read. It's likely, once the current generation dies off, that e-book sales will too, along with the doomed printed book."

"What a sour opinion. Librarians are educators and must meet the public where it is. The younger generation only looks at screens. I'm exaggerating, of course, but not by much. Let's move on. I have some news that should please you. We had a meeting and have agreed to spend whatever is necessary to restore and conserve the plate books in the French Scientists and Savants Collection, about ten percent. They will be used in exhibitions."

"You mean for show."

"There you go again."

That ended the conversation. Michael went home seething. He wanted someone to talk to. That would have been Elizabeth, if things weren't so screwed up. Where was George?

AT WORK MARÍA had stacked his mail and a sheaf of papers in the middle of his desk. These were cataloging worksheets for newly arrived stock. He had trained María to prepare the bibliographic description, which includes the author, title, imprint, pagination, illustrations, binding, dimensions, and physical condition of the book. For antiquarian books, this is exacting work, requiring the application of arcane cataloging principles. He was proud of the way she had caught on. His role was to complete the worksheet by adding an annotation and a price. This division of labor worked well. As he flipped through the worksheets, he was surprised to see that María had herself written the annotations for several titles. The one he was staring at read as follows:

Ximeno, José

Opúsculo sobre los catorce casos reservados y otras tantas excomuniones sinodales del Concilio Mexicano Provincial tercero celebrado en el año 1585 y aprobado en Roma por el Papa Sixto V en 1589. México: Alexandro Valdés, 1816.

251 p., 15 cm., fullbound in tan calf, gilded spine.

A treatise of ecclesiastical law covering fourteen of the most serious mortal sins, including homicide, abortion, the invocation of demons, Black Masses, sacrilegious luxury, perjury, bigamy, blasphemy, incest, sodomy and bestiality, forgery, and arson. Second part covers lesser offenses subject to excommunication, such as printing without a license from the Church or the King. The cases are explained clearly and logically to further the correct administration of the Sacrament of Penance. Provides remarkable insights into 16th-century Mexican society.

Michael took the paper and went out to see María, who was at a worktable wiping dust off some books. He dangled the sheet in front of her.

"This is very good."

She smiled shyly. "I just imitated the way you do it."

"But why?"

"Well, you know, we received that big shipment from your trip to Mexico, and I knew you were preoccupied with other matters, so I was trying to move things along."

"Okay, but you picked such an odd book to start with, a dry legal treatise. Why did it interest you?"

"One of my friends in high school had an abortion. She thought her dad would kill her if he found out she was pregnant. It was awful. She felt scared and depressed and guilty. I remembered her when I was looking through that book after unpacking it. I noticed the section on abortion, and read it. And I wondered who these accused women were who lived 400 years ago, how they got pregnant, and how terrified they must have felt without doctors and clinics in such a superstitious society with the Church always ready to condemn them. It moved me."

"So I see. You certainly wrote it up nicely. Anymore surprises?"

"You think so?"

Perched on her stool, beaming, María Sandoval, Chicana.

~

MICHAEL DECIDED to phone Elizabeth again. "I want to ask you, before you make any final decisions, to read a couple of articles by G. Thomas Tanselle. He's a professor at Columbia and President of the Biblio-graphical Society of the University of Virginia. He carefully explains why reproductions cannot substitute for original primary sources when doing research."

"For some research. I know very well that our project will not please a certain kind of pedant, the bibliophilic scholar. But for an assistant professor of history, stuck in North Dakota without travel funds, being able to access these rare texts online from his own office will be a boon. We will be supporting *his* research. Actually, the decision you refer to has already been made. Digitization will start next month."

"Then I would like to make a final offer. I would like to buy back the collection. I will have to seek financing or pay in installments, but I'm good for it."

"Michael, that's out of the question. Those books belong to the Board of Governors of the University now. They cannot be returned. We are obligated to protect them."

"But you're not protecting them! Just the opposite. You should all be lined up and shot."

7

He decided not to marry, "that manner of life being too thorny and difficult for a man of study." In support he would quote Horace: "Nothing is better than celibate life." Yet he noticed women, such as the young and pretty wife of old Scipio Claramontius, philosopher and mathematician. At the time it was expected that a librarian not marry, but instead be "married" to the library. Naudé preferred a different relationship. He called his library his "daughter." Perhaps he avoided temptations by keeping busy, always being in a hurry, not dallying. Most nights he would go to bed weary. But what about nights when he was keyed up? When his mind was racing?

Michael could not believe the mistake he had made.

He stayed late in his office cursing and railing, until growing tired, he became numb with depression. He stretched out on the couch to doze. As he fell asleep his heart detonated, in a paroxysm. He leaped into darkness. It was death. In seconds he would be dead. He cried "No!" fell back and groaned, wanting to be held. Eyes shut, hair drenched, heart pounding. As he breathed, his pulse slowed, returning to evenness, reclaiming sleep. Later the room got so cold he woke up and went home.

In ten frenetic years, Naudé amassed a library of 40,000 books and manuscripts for Cardinal Mazarin. By comparison, this was three times the size of its closest rival, the Bodleian Library at Oxford. Most titles were acquired on difficult and dangerous buying trips abroad during the Thirty Years' War. In Germany he had to travel with strong escort, fearing capture by enemy raiding parties. Writing to Nicolas de Gremonville, the French Ambassador to Venice, on May 6, 1647, he said that he was an hour away from departing for England, Holland, and Flanders, where the Cardinal was sending him to perfect the library. The day before the King had come to be shown around the palace and library, and the next day the ambassador from Denmark would do the same, following a sumptuous meal. The closer the palace came to completion the more impatient the Cardinal was to see it completed. This was why Naudé worked with all possible diligence. He expected to return in three months.

The use of the word *perfect*, his frequent wish "to bring the library to perfection," suggested that Naudé and his master regarded the library as a work of art, not a never-ending process. He knew better, of course, admitting in the *Advis* that "no one is ever able actually to complete a library."

In the cool freshness of morning, he would walk from his lodgings in the Cour de l'Abbaye Sainte-Geneviève in the Latin Quarter across the river to the palace on the right bank. There were several routes he could take without much changing the distance. It took him forty-five minutes. The library was built on top of the stables where a hundred horses were kept. The architect Pierre Le Muet had read the *Advis*, which recommended locating a library on a middle floor to avoid dampness from the ground and inclemency and heat from above. The early light of the morning passed through eight tall windows, making it easy to see inside the great room. To protect against fire, it was forbidden to light a candle in the library; for the same reason, it was not heated. (One of Naudé's successors was dismissed for incompetence when he was caught breaking this rule.) Naudé's desk was cluttered with correspondence, receipts, ledgers, catalogs, and stacks of books—new acquisitions and those he was using for his own writing. He would display his latest finds on a large table in the middle of the room. The Cardinal wanted to see all of the new purchases before they were classified. Daily, as His Eminence swept through the gallery on the way to chapel, he would stop and leaf through each volume, glancing at the title page and admiring the binding.

In running the library, Naudé concentrated on acquisitions. No catalog from his period has ever been found or cited. He probably never got around to making one, even though his theory called for it. Not enough help, not enough time. More interest in chasing game than dressing it. Besides, he carried everything in his head. *He* was the catalog to the eighty to one hundred persons who used the library on Thursdays when it was open to the public. Books were arranged in alcoves and on shelves according to a broad classification scheme, but after a while sheer numbers and lack of space interfered with order, and they were piled on the floor in proximity to where they belonged. Nevertheless, he could put his finger on just the book wanted or identify a host of diverse sources that bore on a topic. He would bring out books no one else had ever heard of—or only heard of, never seen. So impressive was his erudition that historian and philosopher François de La Mothe Le Vayer called him "the living library."

Early on he had formed the habit of examining books wherever he found them—those owned by his teachers, for sale by booksellers, in the collections of learned and well-to-do acquaintances. Once he ran his eyes over a title page and leafed through a volume, he remembered it. Almost daily he made the rounds of the booksellers, looking for anything new. Not having enough money to buy a fraction of the books he wanted, he read as many as he could standing up. Interesting titles sold out quickly and disappeared. When needed later, they would be virtually unobtainable. Recorded knowledge seemed to be scattering chaotically, away from students and scholars. Books mainly gravitated to places of wealth, but this didn't mean they were either used or cared for. "The treasures of Antiquity," he wrote to his older friend Nicolas Fabri de Peiresc in 1636, "are discovered every day, and God knows that if the Princes took care to look in places where moths and worms are eating them, how many could be put to profit by the Public and by literature."

The churches were no better. When he served Cardinal Bagni in Italy, he wrote: "Several months ago

I began to look at papers in the archive of the cathedral of Riète, and reported to His Eminence that it was in confusion, extremely neglected, and almost entirely consumed by rats and moisture. He ordered me to save what I could, put it in order and inventory it, an occupation that will keep me busy until the third week in Lent." In addition books were censored, suppressed and hidden away at the insistence of the Church and the King. Describing his research for the *Syntagma de studio militari*, he complained:

> I found so many authors who had already written about the ancient and modern military that to satisfy my humor, which is to not repeat what others have said, I go looking for new titles and questions, which causes me a great deal of trouble because I do not have enough books at hand to treat even the simplest questions, and as to those books I can discover among my friends or in public libraries, I have to battle eternally against the humor of the Italians, which is not to lend them, and against excommunication and censorship, which enchains, imprisons, and restricts them so that they can hardly be used.

He always wrote in haste, even when penning important letters to important people. He employed long run-on sentences, and didn't bother to connect the phrases well. Words were left out and subjects switched abruptly. His handwriting was a scrawl, "hieroglyphics" according to a later editor, extremely difficult to decipher. Peiresc said about one message: "It is so badly written and in letters so small that all of my magnifying glasses were too weak, and I have scarcely understood half of it."

Frustrated by the conditions of scholarship, Naudé began to create a library in his head: *une bibliothèque idéale*. At the time there was no record of current publications, and the few retrospective catalogues and bibliographies, such as Conrad Gesner's *Biblioteca universalis* (1545), were expensive, hard to obtain, and dated. Without such tools, he had to rely upon memory, mentally gathering books together by author and by subject. Arguments should be countered by refutations. Spurious works noted. Translations. His mind held a collection that existed nowhere else, which, in its breadth and tolerance, could exist nowhere else. Underlying this unusual collection was a new idea, which he worked out in his famous little treatise. The idea of the public research library. He published the *Advis* at the age of twenty-seven, just a few years after he began practicing librarianship in the service of Henri de Mesmes, President of the Parliament of Paris.

He defined an institution that did not yet exist in order to give himself a goal for his career.

And just what did the *Advis* set down? That first one must collect the classic authors, both ancient and modern, in every field of learning, "chosen from the best editions...along with the best and most learned interpreters and commentators." Moreover, these texts should be available in both their original languages and in translation. Originals are important because of their clarity and richness of conception, and to verify texts or passages that are debated or challenged. Next one should collect books written by experts on a vast number of subjects as well as opponents and critics of these authors, in particular authors disdained "for having set themselves up against the ancients and having learnedly examined what others were used to accept by tradition." First books on a subject are especially to be prized, "since...learning as with water...is never more fair, pure, and limpid than at its source...." Include "all the works of the most learned and famous heretics," because "it is necessary...that our scholars should find these authors somewhere available in order to refute them." Modern authors are to be preferred as much as ancient authors, and neglected authors must not be neglected, "while our new censors or plagiarists take their places and enrich themselves with their stolen clothes." Manuscripts are preferable to printed copies of them. In sum, nothing of research value should be overlooked in building a library, "neither satires, broadsides, theses, scraps, nor proofs." With such a library, a man "may with reason call himself...citizen of the whole world, since with it he may know all...and be ignorant of nothing."

8

"Hey, man, you really are getting worked up about this stuff. Has it occurred to you that you may be the only person in the world who cares?" This from the mouth of a college student nerd they employed to tweak the business website, who was listening in on their conversation. María and Michael turned to look at him. "As seen on TV, this is still an exciting, beautiful world, full of adventure and beer. A car racing across a pristine desert. Your companion: a young, voluptuous woman. Later you will share a drink at sunset. Relax, go with the flow."

María cracked up. Michael shrugged, palms up.

With business still sluggish, they were spending

more time talking. María was also disgusted with what was happening at the university, but not to the same extent as Michael. He had been the one who pounded the pavement looking for those books in several countries for the better part of five years, who pored over booksellers' catalogs, who corresponded with collectors and authorities in the field all over the world. All that work had finally paid off when the widow of a prominent historian of science contacted him about her husband's library. He had flown back to New Haven, rented a car in pouring rain, and found her home on a quiet street. She had invited him to dry out and warm up in the kitchen with a cup of tea and a slice of just-baked nut bread. They chatted for a half-hour. She was a kindly lady probably in her mid-seventies.

In the library, there was a handsome writing table positioned near the window, with the professor's research files and papers neatly shelved on an adjacent wall. There was also a cozy spot for reading, with a comfortable leather armchair, a large side table to pile books and drink on, and a good lamp. Michael noticed a fine French clock and a few engravings, but he was soon dazzled by the surrounding book shelves. There he found Jean de Léry, *Histoire d'un voyage fait en la terre du Brazil* (1578); Charles-Marie de La Condamine, *Journal du voyage fait par ordre du roi à l'équateur* (1751);

Chappe d'Auteroche, *Voyage en Californie pour l'observation du passage de Vénus sur le disque du soleil, le juin 1769* (1772); Alexander von Humboldt, *Voyage aux régions équinoxiales du nouveau continent*, 3 vols (1814-1825); Alcide d'Orbigny, *Voyage dans l'Amérique méridionale*, 9 vols. (1834-1847); Guillermo Dupaix, *Antiquités mexicaines*, 3 vols. (1844); Henri Coudreau, *La France Équinoxiale*, 2 vols. and atlas (1886-1887), and many others. It had taken the professor fifty years to track down these books.

He had made her a fair offer, dismissing any thought of low-balling the value of the collection. He would not try to steal it from her. She was mainly concerned that the books went into the right hands. He assured her that they would.

Once the check had been written, he knew it was time to offer the entire collection for sale. It was ready. For five years he had poured money into the project without return on investment. But he always remained confident he could sell the collection, given its quality, definition, and rarity. George had urged him on, saying that he would find some way of buying it. Now the baby was ready to be delivered.

He felt betrayed that the collection was about to meet a digital fate—and in turn that he had betrayed the widow, the dead professor, and certainly the books themselves. He didn't know what to do, but he couldn't drop it.

Seeing how down he was, María started to bring food in for them to share: homemade tamales and *frijoles*, savored with black coffee. *Pan dulce*. Enchiladas and chiles rellenos. Something different each time.

9

At 7:30 in the morning Michael found a spot in visitor's parking at the university. It was a bright but chilly day. He wore chinos, a sweater, and a heavy field coat. From the backseat he pulled out a large placard on a stick, which read:

STOP THIS LIBRARY FROM
DESTROYING RARE BOOKS

He felt stupid and embarrassed, but he proceeded up the walkway towards the library. He planted himself at the entrance as the doors were opened, and students, a few faculty, and library staff members began to stream in. It didn't take long before people started questioning him. What's going on? Who's doing this?

Why? Who are you? He explained that the library had a large project to digitize a valuable collection of rare books, that in the process many would be disbound and damaged, that only a few of them would be restored with the greater part being consigned to cold storage inaccessible to the public, who would be left with nothing more than an image on a computer screen.

Some people were shocked, some shrugged. A few apparently marched right to the office of the library director (who hadn't arrived yet) to protest. When Elizabeth came to work and saw him, she stopped dead, raised her hand to her mouth, then rushed up, feverishly whispering: "Michael, what are you doing? You're making a fool of yourself. You're embarrassing the Library. You're embarrassing me. Stop this."

"I tried to stop it, but you weren't interested."

"You are completely misrepresenting what we are trying to do."

"No, you explained it to me quite clearly. Now I am merely telling the public."

She pushed by him and entered the library. It didn't take long for the campus police to arrive. They made him get out his ID, and took down the particulars. They asked him what he was doing. What his connection to the university was. They warned him about obstructing traffic, damaging property, or causing trouble. They told him that he could not enter the library with the sign. For a while one cop hung around watching. Just before noon a student reporter from the campus daily showed up. She took his picture as well as a lot of notes.

Michael answered questions all day long. He told people to let the library know if they were concerned. He also got some flack from a group of computer science students who said he was resisting modernization. About 4:00 PM he went home, completely bushed. He phoned María to tell her what he was doing, and she squealed with delight. *"¡Qué hombre!* Go get 'em, *ése."*

The next morning he again stationed himself at the door of the library. To his astonishment he was soon joined by another picketer, a tall, thin, scraggly-bearded graduate student in English. His sign read:

LIBRARIANS:
THE ENEMIES OF BOOKS

Michael was overjoyed by the support, but said that he thought the sign might be going a little too far. The student replied, "No, no, it's an old controversy. In the eighteenth century Edward Young said:

Unlearned men of books assume the care,
As eunuchs are the guardians of the fair.

"Well, I would hardly call librarians ignorant. Many of them hold advanced degrees."

"True, but something has gone awry in Library-land. I have an inside source, who shall remain nameless, but who fills me in. The modern librarian is basically a shill for the Info Industry. It's a shame that tax and tuition payers still have to bear the cost of their salaries, which more properly should be paid by their corporate masters. Their so-called business and contract negotiations with predatory electronic publishers for obscenely expensive databases, electronic journals, and e-books are little more than mating rituals. But in the end there's no question who remains the dominant partner flying ever higher, and who's left to sit on the eggs."

Michael was speechless. A little scooter truck pulled up with a stack of student newspapers for the kiosk. His picture was on the front page, the headline reading:

BOOKSELLER PROTESTS BIBLIOCLASM

Whew, he thought, that reporter must be an English major too. But she defined the word, and the article was good. Two members of the Faculty Library Committee came by and asked probing questions. Finally, one acknowledged that the Library Director had informed them of the digitization project, but apparently had skipped over a number of details.

Around noon Elizabeth briskly exited the building, hissing, "Do you know that you are ruining my career?"

AFTER THE *LOS ANGELES TIMES* picked up the story, the library announced that it was postponing the project. For further study. It strongly protested the implication that the project was not in the service of scholarship, which increasingly was being carried on electronically.

Michael was elated, and María decided to throw an impromptu party at the office. She invited several bookseller friends, the graduate student who came with his girlfriend (a young librarian), the postman, her own mother, and her daughter. Champagne flowed, food was gobbled, toasts were offered. And because it was a celebration, María, for the first time since she was interviewed for the job, wore a dress, a dress that a Chicana would wear to dance in, maddeningly sexy.

10

It was probably the happiest period of his life. The Cardinal's library had grown large and was thrown open to the public. Indeed, their demands kept him so busy that he complained about no longer having time to write books of his own. He found himself fetching volumes and answering questions to distraction. In a moment of self-pity he recalled a famous little story from *The Travels of Friar Odoric of Pordenone* who journeyed to China in the fourteenth century. There the friar saw men who fish with trained birds, with cormorants. The fisherman fastens a metal ring around the bird's neck, which in turn is tied to a long cord. He lets the bird soar and fly around and dive for fish, but when it catches one, the ring prevents it from swallowing. The bird only tastes the fish, as a librarian only tastes knowledge.

But he wouldn't let an occasional defeatist thought interfere with his work. Did its audacity sometimes unsettle him? He had learned in Italy, amidst the constant machinations of the palace inhabitants, to keep tight lipped. What he was attempting was nothing less than a direct application of Bacon's principle that knowledge is power. He would elevate the library, formerly a rich man's ornament, to an instrument of state, where the ruler could seek superior advice based on a review and analysis of pertinent literature.

Financially comfortable for the first time in his life, Naudé bought a little country villa outside of Paris in the village of Gentilly, where he and his friends gathered to dine and discourse, old actors of an ancient dialogue. His friend Guy Patin described one such weekend:

> Monsieur Gassendi and I have been invited to dinner and to spend the night at his house, on condition that we have a debauchery. But God knows what kind! Monsieur Naudé only drinks water and has never tasted wine. Monsieur Gassendi's health is so delicate that he dares not drink, and imagines that his body

would burst into flames if he did. As for me I can only sprinkle pounce on the writing of these two great men. I drink very little. Nevertheless, it will be a debauchery, but the philosophic kind, and perhaps something more. Perhaps we three, cured of hobgoblins and freed from the trouble of scruples, which tyrannize consciences, may draw quite near to the sanctuary.

Away from hectic Paris, away from prying ears, in the beauty of the country, life was sweet—until the wheel again turned.

In 1648, just as the Thirty Years' War in Europe was winding down, civil war in France broke out, largely to protest the crushing taxation needed to prosecute the seemingly endless war. The Parliament of Paris, joined by six provincial parliaments, demanded a reduction in taxes, as well as the right to approve new ones and to debate and modify royal decrees. They also demanded the suppression of the Intendants, powerful provincial officials appointed by the monarchy, who administered police, judicial, and financial matters.

This uprising, which occurred during the minority of Louis XIV, had three distinct phases and lasted five years. It was called the *Fronde*, a word which means "slingshot," so named because of the capricious and selfish behavior of the participants. Everyone got involved: the bourgeoisie, the aristocracy, the armies, the street rabble. High-ranking women stirred the pot vigorously. The one person all of them could agree on hating was First Minister Cardinal Jules Mazarin.

There were good reasons, of course. Besides the squeeze of taxation, Mazarin's policies had led to price deflation and widespread unemployment. And, worse, he was a foreigner who had never learned to pronounce the French language correctly. An Italian *buffone*.

The attack began with a swarm of pamphlets, broadsides, rhymes, and songs—called *mazarinades*—which grew in number to more than five thousand titles. They were sold on the street and on the bridges spanning the Seine, fanned out on the pavement like cards in a game of chance. Naudé collected them, and when he had a fist full, had them bound into volumes. He urged his master to suppress their publication, but was ignored. Finally, he took action himself, writing a 718-page rebuttal to the slander called *Jugement de tout ce qui a esté imprimé contre le Cardinal Mazarin*. This had no effect.

Fleeing the city, the royal family and Mazarin took up residence in Saint Germain, a fortified castle four leagues away. A delegation from the Parliament of Paris pursued them with a demand that Mazarin be expelled. These men were kept waiting in a cold rain for more than two hours and then rebuffed. Furious, the Parliament issued orders to defend the city. To pay for this costly action they resolved to sell all of the opulent furnishings in the Cardinal's palace—except for the library, which was placed under the sworn custody of Naudé. Apprehensive, he wrote the Cardinal recommending that he give the library to the university to save it from an impending "shipwreck."

The Monarchy made concessions, and was asked to return, but in less than two years the inconclusive truce fell apart. This prompted Jacques Tubeuf, President of the Chamber of Accounts, to repossess the Cardinal's palace as security against debts still owed. His motive was actually to save it for the Cardinal, his friend. Solemnly, Naudé turned over the keys to the library, taking leave with tearing eyes.

Mazarin again slipped out of the city, this time to stay with the Archbishop of Cologne. On December 29, 1651, the Parliament issued an *arrêt* ordering "that the library and furnishings of the Cardinal be sold, preferably for the sum of 150,000 francs, which will be given to the one who brings the Cardinal to justice, dead or alive."

In full panic, Naudé wrote to the Parliament, pleading:

> For me who cherishes it as a work of my hands and the miracle of my life, I avow to you ingenuously that, since you hurled the lightening bolt from the heaven of your justice on this work so rare, so beautiful, and so excellent, which I have by my vigils and labors brought to such perfection that one could not morally desire greater, I have been dumbfounded and astonished....
>
> Messieurs, it is composed of more than 40,000 volumes, sent by Kings and Princes of Europe as well as by French Ambassadors who have journeyed to distant lands. To say that I have traveled to Flanders, Italy, England, and Germany to bring back what was most beautiful and rare is a small thing in comparison to the pains taken by these crowned heads to favor the praiseworthy designs of His Eminence....
>
> Strange thing, Messieurs, that the best furnished lawyers are constrained to confess their poverty when they see the great collection of books of their profession that I have made in this rich library; that the greatest accumulation of volumes in medicine is nothing in comparison to what I have assembled in this faculty; that philosophy is more beautiful and

thriving than it ever was in Greece; that the Italians, Germans, Spanish, English, Polish, Dutch, and other nations find their histories much richer and better supplied than in their own countries; that Catholics and Protestants can verify all sorts of passages and resolve all sorts of difficulties.... It is the eighth wonder of the world....

Can you permit, Messieurs, for the public to be deprived of a thing so useful and so precious? Can you endure that this lovely flower, already spreading its fragrance to everyone, withers in your hands?...

Please believe, the ruin of this library will be more carefully marked in all histories and calendars than was ever the conquest and sacking of Constantinople.

No one listened. A week later he was summoned to the library at 10:00 AM, where he found three sales commissioners—Messieurs Portail, Pithou, and Petau —in the room with the medical books. While they looked around they said nothing of significance to him, and he wondered why he had been asked to come. Monsieur Portail railed against the Cardinal for not having made peace and for laying siege to Paris and Bordeaux. Finally, he announced that they would start selling off the library the next day, beginning with the bibles, which were the best. Naudé countered that they should start with duplicate volumes, to do the least harm.

At 8:00 AM the next morning he persuaded three booksellers, who were assisting with the sale, to package the duplicates into lots. However, at 11:00 AM, Monsieur Portail became aware of what they were doing, ordered everyone to stop, and yelling and swaggering told them that he was the master. Then speaking directly to Naudé, he said that he would not be taking advice from anyone, that the more Naudé said, the less he would do, in fact he would do completely the opposite. He would start with the bibles and sell half the library by the end of the day.

All of this, and what follows, Naudé recounted in long, desperate letters to Mazarin.

At 2:00 PM the sale began. A large crowd had been prowling the library like rats, some looking, some putting books aside, some stealing. A man named Le Blanc, who happened to be the Cardinal's prosecutor of debtors, offered to take the entire library for 40,000 livres. When they said that the amount was not reasonable, he raised it to 50,000. But Monsieur Portail mocked him, saying that the time to buy in gross had passed, and that he wished to sell in pieces.

And so, the great bible of Monsieur Le Gay went in

an instant for 365 livres, followed by that of Anvers in eight volumes for 300 livres, and so on.

Fleeing the library, Naudé frantically sought out persons of influence, hoping they would intervene or at least temper Monsieur Portail's furious humor. Most of them could not be found, and few offered help. He himself had been barred from further attendance at the sale, so he sent two men to observe. They reported rampant theft. Monsieur Pithou took books from the library two or three times a day, employing his clerk, the tutor of his children, and his valet to haul them away in carriages. He must have been a deeply religious man, for he had almost all the bibles. Monsieur Petau had the booksellers make up lots for him, asking:

"How much is it worth?"

"Is it for you, Monsieur?"

"Yes. It can't be worth much. How much do you estimate?"

"Whatever you like, Monsieur."

Monsieur Portail said "I don't know good books. Tell me if these are good." He had them carried to the chapel, which was guarded by the bailiff. When night came and everyone had left, he entered the sale into the official record, saying "You see, I take nothing that I don't buy." Another time his valet was caught sneaking books out under his cloak, for which he received a good pummeling. Monsieur Portail rushed up, "You are affronting my servant! I am barely able to resist taking you prisoner."

Even with the assist of thievery, it took six weeks to complete the sale and empty the great library. Queen Christina of Sweden, through an agent, bought all of the manuscripts for 6,000 livres. And Naudé, reverting to his original profession, bought all of the medicine for 3,900 livres. Hearing the fatal news, Mazarin said that he had lost his love for this thing which had cost him so much money and effort to assemble.

Naudé pleaded with the Cardinal not to be so cold. He urged him to dream of reestablishing the library so as not to deprive the people, who had nothing to do with its destruction, of a treasure so precious. "If the city would remain peaceful, I would begin tomorrow to rebuild this marvel, starting with no more than the books I have managed to save."

Without employment, Naudé found himself at loose ends and unable to pay his bills. In addition he was shunned by acquaintances, who knew that he was an unrepentant loyalist. He entered a period of silence. Far to the north, however, Queen Christina saw another opportunity to improve her library. In her own hand, she wrote him, offering the position of Royal Librarian. She promised him excellent remuneration and absolute control of the library, which was bulging with new acquisitions, many taken by conquest. How could Naudé not be flattered, especially at this low ebb in his life? Yet he did not immediately accept, and waited nearly three months before asking the Cardinal's permission. Not offended, Mazarin granted him a leave of absence and even added a letter of recommendation. Quickly Naudé put his affairs in the hands of his brother, and on July 21, 1652, departed for Sweden accompanied by two other men, an antiquarian and an apothecary, also with job offers.

To the consternation of her countrymen, the young, virgin, polymath Queen was engaged in a French brain drain, Descartes having been her greatest catch. It took two months for these men to reach Stockholm by carriage, horseback, and ship. When they arrived, they were pleasantly surprised. The weather was still relatively mild, and the city, while rustic, was neat as a pin. They were temporarily lodged in a comfortable hotel with other scholars, all of whom spoke French. Naudé brightened at the prospect that he would not even need to learn the native tongue.

His first audience with the Queen went splendidly, most of it taking place informally in her wardrobe, where she handed him the keys to the library. The brilliant, bawdy Christina enjoyed playful repartee. Indeed, she had been persuaded by her court physician, Abbé Bourdelot, to reduce her hours of study, to take more baths, to partake in entertainments, and to eat light meals, especially chicken soup, as a cure for her fevers and melancholia. The success of this regime had made the Abbé her court favorite.

Naudé found the library rich in manuscripts but rather spotty in books. Nonetheless, it had completely outgrown its quarters, and a new library was under construction. Most of the volumes were piled on the floor in no particular order. His main job was to catalog and classify them. He worked diligently during the day and seemed to enjoy his after hours in the hotel talking and dining with his erudite friends, who were all engaged in research and writing. Since it was winter, it was best to stay inside. On the whole, an agreeable life, a time to recuperate—until, without warning, a strange incident spoiled it.

One of the men at the hotel, Marcus Meibom, had come to Sweden from Germany to present his book, *Seven Writers on Ancient Music*, to the Queen. He also hoped to become her tutor in Greek. He was twenty-two years old, stocky, and rather unrefined in manners. His presence triggered a malicious idea in the restless mind of Abbé Bourdelot, who delighted in playing practical jokes ostensibly to entertain the Queen. Whispering in her ear during full court, he induced her to ask Meibom to sing a few songs from his book and to have the learned Naudé accompany him with a performance of Greek and Roman dances. This royal desire came so suddenly that the startled men found it impossible to make excuses or refuse, and of course they made fools of themselves, since neither was prepared nor had talent. The court broke up in laughter. Meibom was especially shocked, and his humiliation turned into rage. Afterwards, he asked Bourdelot to step into the library, and beat his face in. Then he fled.

Naudé departed as well. The Cardinal, again in full power, had called him back into service. Naudé was thrilled with the idea of reestablishing the library. He began the journey home in the company of the French ambassador, but on the way contracted a continuous fever and died in Abbeville near the coast of Picardie July 29, 1653, at the age of fifty-three. Before death, he dictated his will and took the sacraments. He was interred in the nave of the Eglise de Saint Georges before the Crucifix.

In his will, Naudé left Mazarin the works of Jean Hus and Hiérosme de Prague, which had been impossible to find while he was His Eminence's librarian. Two packages were on their way from Sweden. Thus he filled what he deemed a serious lack. Even the

largest library has lacks—is forever incomplete. Yet
Naudé and Mazarin strove to "perfect" their library as
though each volume added to its radiance. Naudé's job
was done. Others would have to continue the work. But
in fact no one else has ever come along who was as
good.

11

"Right now I would grade your business C+," Barney said as he squeezed papers and file folders back into his briefcase. "You've paid off your major debts, you have a small cash reserve, and income slightly exceeds expenses. The trouble is, except for the two big collections you sold, sales have been declining. When the lease on this building goes up, you'll start hurting."

Michael didn't really know what to do. He sat at his desk trying to put the pieces together. When he thought about what drew him to this business, it wasn't so much a love of books as a love of reading. Of course the two were inextricably linked. But reading was the more important matter. Public opinion surveys indicated that reading was in decline, particularly among the young.

This failed to explain why the chain bookstores were jammed, or why Amazon.com continued to flourish. Maybe their customers were merely buying cookbooks or some such. Or maybe it was the last hurrah of diehards. He wondered what the world was going be like with fewer and fewer readers. Day-to-day changes were almost imperceptible, like with global warming, but he sensed a steady dumbing down. Fewer people cared about getting it right. When reading is abandoned, one loses a way of knowledge, the kind produced from sequential thinking. Starting at the beginning, proceeding through the middle, and concluding at the end—a structure required whether it's fiction, philosophy, or science. The opposite of a swarm of sound bites and sight bites, of web surfing and hypertextual wandering. The sheer quantity of material passing across TV and computer screens ensured its mediocrity. Thank God for *Harry Potter*. He caused millions of kids to read big thick books again. Could it be habit forming?

The old-time bookseller, where did he go? Cranky, cynical, eccentric, irreverent, but oh so knowledgeable —formerly an indispensable agent in building great library collections. A demiurge, a counselor, even a magician when he found desperately needed books.

With rare exceptions, librarians withdrew the welcome mat for his ilk quite some time ago. Did he scare them?

Now many libraries were poised to take the next step: to stop buying printed books entirely, except as museum objects for special collections, the occasional "show book." The rub was that readers still seemed to prefer the printed kind, which left the e-book to incipient nonreaders, a large but unreliable constituency. Why it was necessary to pick on the book—a technological, ergonomic, and aesthetic marvel—only the info-infernal could explain. But, unquestionably, for Corporate America there was a lot of money to be made.

He thought of Naudé and the destruction of the library. His was a tragedy. The way it was happening in our day, a farce. No nefarious agenda, but a similar result. A fade-out of human memory. He believed he might be able to survive by selling his goods facelessly on the Internet. In any case he didn't have a Plan B for his life. He expected to be a bookseller—a *librero*—till the end.

12

There is little more to say, except that a few days later George phoned. He had heard that his former employers were giving Michael a hard time, and that Michael had paid back in kind. "Bravo. Your antics even made the *Boston Globe*." George was now working in a Jesuit college. "A big cut in pay, but otherwise I like it. The Jesuits still read books." The reason he phoned was to invite Michael to join him on a dig in Guatemala, which he could view either as a little vacation or as a chance to do some real work. "As for libraries, unless the pendulum swings back, guys like us are finished. I don't know what we can do about it. It's up to readers. They will have to draw a line in the sand. And if they can't get rid of the usurpers, they may have to reinvent the institution, as Benjamin Franklin did. If this sounds hopeless, remember that libraries are centripetal. Even small ones can be good ones. I say let the aliterates stay plugged in to the electronic library, clicking their mouses, channel surfing, zooming around swarming galaxies of information, shopping sites, and car chases. For the rest of us, the Bard's advice is still the best: 'Come, and take choice of all my library, and so beguile thy sorrow.' So, take his advice: 'Beguile thy sorrow.'"

Michael hung up the phone, shaking his head but smiling broadly. He looked around at all his books, then swiftly stood and nearly skipped into the outer office where María was tidying up her desk before going home.

"María, do you think your mom could baby-sit Teresa tonight?"

"Why?"

"Because I would like to ask you to have dinner with me."

"What's the occasion?"

"You are."

"Me?"

"Yes."

"If I do, it means I won't be calling you 'Boss' anymore."

"No."

"You finally noticed."

NOTES

Among the sources I drew on to write this fiction, specifically the parts about Gabriel Naudé, were *Gabriel Naudé, 1600-1653* by Jack A. Clarke (1970) and *Histoire de la Bibliothèque Mazarine et du Palais de l'Institut* by Alfred Franklin (1901). These are respectively the best biography of the librarian and the best history of the library. I also used correspondence by Naudé and his contemporaries found in *Lettres de Naudé à Gremonville,* edited by Kathryn Willis Wolfe and Phillip J. Wolfe (1986); *Les Correspondants de Peiresc: lettres inédites*, edited by Philippe Tamizey de Larroque, 2 vols. (1879-1897; reprinted 1972); *Lettres de Gabriel Naudé à Jacques Dupuy (1632-1652)*, edited by Phillip Wolfe (1982); *Considérations politiques sur le Fronde: La Correspondance entre Gabriel Naudé et le Cardinal Mazarin,* edited by Kathryn Willis

Wolfe and Phillip J. Wolfe (1991); *Lettres de Gui Patin*, edited by J.-H. Reveillé-Parise, 3 vols. (1846); and *Opera Omnia* by Pierre Gassendi, 6 vols. (1658; reprinted 1964).

A contemporary ana, *Naudaeana et Patiniana: ou singularitez remarquables, prises des conversations de Mess. Naudé & Patin*, 2nd. ed., rev., corr. & augm. (1703), was another wellspring. Translations and paraphrases were made by the author, except for brief quotations on library collection development principles, which came from Naudé's *Advice on Establishing a Library*, translated by Archer Taylor (1950). The Swedish episode was described in *Memoires concernant Christine, Reine de Suède* by Johan Arckenholtz, 4 vols. (1751-1760). It was the 17th-century philosopher Pierre Bayle who called Naudé "the best-read man in France."

ACKNOWLEDGMENTS

Several friends (librarians, booksellers, professors, writers, and a heart surgeon) were kind enough to read this story in an earlier version. Their diverse comments were invaluable. I thank all of them: Judith Auth, Sidney Berger, John Bloomberg-Rissman, Michael Burgess, Paul Damus, Howard Karno, Larry Lauerhass, Leland Lubinsky, Bob Nardini, and Douglas Rees. Later, Sarah Hoenicke Flores edited the text with great skill, and my daughter, Adriana Briscoe, a biology professor and essayist, suggested finishing touches. Above all, I thank my wife Lori, who was my first reader, late one night.

ABOUT THE AUTHOR

Peter Briscoe has had the pleasure not only of living with books as a reader but also of making them his life's work as a librarian and writer. For more than 30 years he built library collections at two universities. A specialist in collection development, book acquisitions, special collections, and preservation, he directed efforts that led to the purchase or donation of 1.5 million volumes from all over the world on nearly all subjects. He loved his job but increasingly worried about the fate of books and reading in a digital, post-literate world. Briscoe, who attained the rank of Distinguished Librarian at the University of California, Riverside, and subsequently that of Associate University Librarian, is now Emeritus. He is the author or co-author of five books, including a translation from the French of José Cabanis' novel, *Night Games* (1993), *Reading the Map of Knowledge: The Art of Being a Librarian* (2001), *Mexico at the Hour of Combat* (2012), and *The Bookseller: Stories* (2022).